Advance Praise
The Spoils

"*The Spoils* is a gritty and addictive debut, a wild ride of ill-fated grifts and characters attempting to shrug off their bad luck with even worse choices. Pycior's stories crackle with wit and humanity and are an absolute pleasure."

—John Jodzio,
author of *Knockout* and *If You Lived Here You'd Already Be Home*

"In 'Preservation,' a boy who has recently lost his mother visits a museum dedicated to the treasures of a once-sunken Missouri steamboat. His favorite artifact is the walnut tree trunk that brought the ship to ruin. 'It's like ... the snag is the most important thing,' he tells his father. Casey Pycior's characters are adrift in a sea of alcohol, drugs, separations, infidelities, and divorces: a carpenter who follows disasters, and is one himself; a tow-truck driver who is a wreck; a live-in surrogate dad who can't fix his addicted girlfriend, but can fix a faucet at 3 a.m.; a Generals basketball player paid to lose every game to the Harlem Globetrotters. All of them hit a 'snag,' and the characters go deep, some desperate and flailing, some resilient and triumphant. In *The Spoils*, Pycior's narrations and narrators give us storytelling at its very best—honest and steady, heartfelt and true."

—Thomas Fox Averill, O. Henry Award winner,
author of *A Carol Dickens Christmas*, *rode*, and
Secrets of the Tsil Café

"Casey Pycior's collection *The Spoils* contains an achingly observed collection of characters, scrabbling for their dreams on the edges of the Great Plains. These strivers often leave blood and treachery in their wake, but Pycior's strength is the intricate craftsmanship he employs to illuminate each soul. Think Tobias Wolff in Wichita, or William Trevor in Kansas City—but above all, read this book and discover its remarkable pleasures for yourself. I did, and I think *The Spoils* announces a thrilling new voice in American fiction.

—Whitney Terrell,
author of *The Good Lieutenant*

"Casey Pycior writes stories you won't soon forget. This fine collection features an arresting cast of characters down on their luck, money, and themselves. Still, they continue to search for peace, redemption, or the smallest victory. Thankfully, whether the characters win or lose, we are rewarded by each character's memorable, emotional journey. To the reader goes *The Spoils*."

—Cote Smith,
author of *Hurt People*

"Casey Pycior's debut collection, *The Spoils*, is one of the best I've read in a long time. In tough, unadorned prose, he captures the raw, attenuated lives of the men and women struggling to exist on the fringes of society, economically and socially, isolated as they are in the Midwest. Reminiscent of the best of early Hemingway in the way he examines and imparts depth and meaning to the small gestures of individuals who despite their efforts at connection in love, must continue to exist in the face of the disappointment and loss that is most often their fate. What moves the reader is Pycior's ability to lay bare the most hidden dreams and elemental desires of his characters, lifting them with the delicate touch of a scalpel opening the chest to reveal the beating heart, partially ruined, but worthy of our care and attention."

—Jonis Agee,
author of *The Bones of Paradise* and *The River Wife*

THE SPOILS

THE SPOILS

stories

CASEY PYCIOR

SWITCHGRASS BOOKS
NORTHERN ILLINOIS UNIVERSITY PRESS   DEKALB IL

Published by Switchgrass Books, an imprint of Northern Illinois University Press
Northern Illinois University Press, DeKalb 60115
© 2017 Casey Pycior
All rights reserved
Printed in the United States of America
26 25 24 23 22 21 20 19 18 17   1 2 3 4 5
978-0-87580-761-4 (paper)
978-1-60909-216-0 (e-book)
Book and cover design by Yuni Dorr
Trophy in cover photo donated by Hirschbein Trophies, Sycamore, Illinois

Excerpt from "Bulldozers and Dirt," words by Patterson Hood, music by Drive-By Truckers, copyright Soul Dump Music (BMI). All rights reserved. Used by permission.

Library of Congress Cataloging-in-Publication Data
Names: Pycior, Casey author.
Title: The spoils : stories / Casey Pycior.
Description: DeKalb, IL : NIU Press, [2017]
Identifiers: LCCN 2016055170 (print) | LCCN 2017004120 (ebook) | ISBN 9780875807164 (pbk. : alk. paper) | ISBN 9781609092160 (e-book) | ISBN 9781609092160 (ebook)
Subjects: LCSH: Men—Fiction. | Middle West—Fiction.
Classification: LCC PS3616.Y43 A6 2017 (print) | LCC PS3616.Y43 (ebook) | DDC 813/.6—dc23
LC record available at https://lccn.loc.gov/2016055170

For my son, Carver, and my wife, Janell:

Carver, know that these stories are for you (even
if they might not always seem like it)

Janell, know that these stories are because of you (even
if they might not always seem like it)

CONTENTS

ACKNOWLEDGMENTS

Few, if any, writers are self-made, and I perhaps more than others owe a debt of gratitude to all the people who helped me to get here. There are too many people to name, but I'll try . . .

First I want to thank my parents, Steve and Debbie, for being there for me always; without them I wouldn't have become the person am I and therefore wouldn't have been able to write these stories.

Thanks, as well, to the rest of my family and to Larry and Marlyn Mohme for their support.

I was in school a long, *long* time (just ask my wife), and had the great fortune to be taught by amazing professors at every step of the way. My very first English professor, Tyler Blake, deserves mention here because if it weren't for his encouragement early on, there is no way I'm doing what I am today, so thank you. Though I hadn't yet admitted (or committed) to writing stories while a graduate student at the University of Missouri-Kansas City, it was there that I first witnessed up close what it means to be a working writer, and the examples those writers, namely Michael Pritchett, Whitney Terrell, Michelle Boisseau, and Christie Hodgen, set have stuck with me to this day. Working on my MFA at Wichita State University was far and away the most formative experience in my writing career. The atmosphere and my professors, Margaret Dawe, Richard Spilman, the late Stephen Hathaway, and Darren DeFrain, were exactly what I needed when I needed them. The germs for a few of the stories in this book began there, and I cannot thank each of you enough for your expertise and generosity. An extra-special thanks to Darren DeFrain for not just being a mentor to me but a good friend. This book first came together while I was the University of Nebraska-Lincoln. Many thanks to Jonis Agee for having unwavering belief in this book and my writing, and to Timothy Schaffert, Joy Castro, and Ted Kooser for being the brilliant writers and teachers you are. To all my former professors, I hope I'm able to impact students' lives the way each of you have impacted mine.

To the fine editors of the literary journals who originally published these stories, your acceptance and encouragement nurtured my confidence and nourished my resolve to keep sending stories out. Thank you.

A huge thank you to Patterson Hood and the rest of the guys in the Drive-By Truckers for granting me permission to use their lyrics in "Disaster Carpenter" . . . and for being arguably the best band America.

A number of classmates and colleagues read, commented, or otherwise supported the writing of the stories in this book (some of them multiple times): Jennifer Bryan, Jordan Farmer, Megan Gannon, Chris Harding-Thornton, Gabe Houck, and Ryan Oberhelman, great writers each. Thank you. Others have offered friendship and encouragement along the way: Connie May Fowler, Stephen Amidon, Scott Blackwood, Dan and Sarah Hoyt, Melinda DeFrain, Sean Doolittle, Charles Dodd White, Marcus Meade, and very old friends, Scott Lero and Travis Elmer. Thanks to all of you.

To my literary brothers, Matt Mulienburg and Brian Seemann: my name is on the cover of this book, but the best of the stories inside it exist in large part to your sharp insights and feedback. I quite literally couldn't have done it without the two of you. No one knows my writing like you guys, and I wouldn't have it any other way. Sharing work with you is what makes writing fun. Let's not stop anytime soon, okay?

Thank you to Linda Manning for taking a chance on this book and championing it; for that I'm forever grateful. And thanks to Nathan Holmes, Lori Propheter, Amy Farranto, Yuni Dorr (for the amazing cover design), and everyone at Switchgrass for all your hard work on my behalf; it means the world to me.

To my son, Carver: this book, like everything else, is for you. You've changed my life in every way, and I'm a better person and a better writer because of you. I hope that when you are old enough to read and understand these stories, you'll be proud that your dad wrote them.

Finally, to Janell . . . honestly, there's not space enough here or in any ten acknowledgments pages to sufficiently thank you for going on this journey with me and making the sacrifices my career has asked of us the last ten years. I hope this book in some way tips the scales. I couldn't—wouldn't—have done any of it without you.

I gratefully acknowledge the publications where many of these stories first appeared (some in slightly different form): "Outing" in *Wigleaf*; "Disaster Carpenter" in *Stuck in the Middle: Writing that Holds You in Suspense*, Main Street Rag; "Home Shopping" in *REAL* 35.2, reprinted in *Redux*; "Preservation" in *Crab Orchard Review* 21; "Absolution" (originally titled "The Video") in *Flash in the Attic 2*, Fiction Attic Press; "If There Could've Been Another Way, I Wish That's How It'd Been" in *Wisconsin Review* 49.2; "Pinchbeck" in *Pear Noir!* 10; "Luck" in *Beloit Fiction Journal* 27; "Chasing a Leak" in *The MacGuffin* 32.3; "The Current" in *Big Muddy* 12.2; "De Facto Romance" in *Storyglossia* 48; "Cashing In" in *Yalobusha Review* 23; "Through the Gears" in *Midwestern Gothic* 13; "As Much as One Deserves" (originally titled "Where I Am and Where I Need to Go") in *Harpur Palate* 14.1; and "The Spoils" in *Front Porch Journal* 23.

STORIES

OUTING

Once, years ago, I spent the day with a woman in a small town outside Kansas City. We hadn't been dating long and didn't know each other well, but we'd just had a scare and somehow thought this outing would be a kind of litmus test for our relationship, or whatever it was we were doing.

At a kitschy winery we sampled every wine they had and, feeling guilty, bought a bottle called "Twister" and took it with us to a (regionally) famous writer's house we learned about from a brochure. Neither of us had read any of the author's work, so much of the self-guided tour of the shabby Victorian was lost on us. We spent an hour beneath a large sycamore behind the house, drinking the sweet wine and joking about a photo of the author reading in the bathtub, his knees, head, and smooth belly poking from the water like that famous photo of the Loch Ness Monster.

As we were leaving, we came to a four-way stop in a neighborhood not far from the author's house. Just as I was about to accelerate, a young boy, no more than two years old and naked from the waist down, wandered out into the street in front of us. I looked at the woman I was with, and her face, rosy from the wine, went slack and her mouth hung open. There was no one in any of the yards on the corners, no one walking on the sidewalk, and no one in any cars on the street. We were alone, together. The boy toddled past the front of the car, smiling the whole time. When he made it across, the woman and I looked at each other again. She reached for my hand resting on the console and squeezed it. I gunned it through the intersection, tires chirping on the pavement.

In the rearview mirror, the boy stopped and turned in our direction. I watched as he got smaller and smaller until I could no longer see him. Later, still gripping my hand, the woman cried as I drove.

I wonder sometimes, when it's late at night and she's in a lover's bed, does she tell this story the same as I do?

DISASTER CARPENTER

Of all the places in the world, I had to go and cut my finger off in Wahoo-fucking-Nebraska.

I'd been working on a crew rebuilding part of a suburb south of Omaha that got tornadoed. I've been all over: Kansas, Missouri, Iowa, Oklahoma, Texas, even down on the Gulf rebuilding after Hurricane Whoever happened to roll through. I guess you could say I'm a disaster carpenter. It's a good life for me. No permanent address, no taxes, and I get to move around and see different parts of the country.

After we finished the job, Steve asked if I wanted to stick with his crew for the next one, a small old-folks home on the outskirts of Wahoo, a town of a couple thousand people, thirty miles west of Omaha. "Six-fifty a week," Steve had said. "Cash money." I usually make a point of not working for the same guy on more than one job, but Steve paid good, at least for someone like me, and he didn't ask questions. Hell, if he asked questions of every guy he hired, he wouldn't have anyone working for him. Sure, for the kind of work I was doing, I could've probably gotten more if it hadn't been under the table. I'm a good carpenter, but not so good I can't be replaced, and Steve, or any other foreman, knows I know this. I'm not qualified for anything else, and it's not as if I could just leave and get some other kind of job, especially not one where I'd make this much. Plus, I don't want anyone to know where I am. If I work on the books, then I have to provide an address, pay taxes, what-have-you, and I can't do that right now. I know what you're thinking, *Oooh, he must be a bad guy.* I'm not—well, at least not that bad, not bad like you're probably thinking. I owe some money, okay. To the courts. For child support. I know, I *know*, I'm a dick, dodging my responsibilities as a father and all that. I get it, trust me. But if I'd have stuck around, man, the way her mom and I used to go at it, my daughter'd be all sorts of fucked up. She might not ever know it, but I did her a favor. Sounds like bullshit, I'm sure, but I think about her every day. I do. I send money when I can, too, but the real shit of it is, my ex won't let me off the hook and marry the guy she's been with for years and let him adopt our daughter. I just can't stand some judge telling me when and how much I have to pay, garnishing my wages and shit.

I took Steve up on his offer to stick with his crew, and it seemed like a good idea at the time. That was four weeks ago. I got a room at the Big Chief Motel, a real shit-hole of a place for transients and life-on-the-road/running-from-the-law types: seven stand-alone huts barely big enough for a rock-hard twin mattress and a press-board dresser/TV stand combo. I only stayed there because it's cheap: $25 a day or $150 a week. It's right on the edge of Wahoo, about a mile from the center of the little Main Street. The sign is a Cleveland Indians Chief Wahoo logo rip-off. I'm sure the owner is committing some kind of crime, copyright infringement or something, but who the hell's going to do anything? There were a couple of other guys on the crew that needed to lay low like me, some with bench warrants, but they commuted from Omaha every morning, so at the end of the workday, I was all by myself out here.

It was one of those guys, Chad, who owes me a goddamn finger. We were laying the sheeting on the roof of one of the units, and I was working on cutting the plywood to fit one of the two dormers when the wind picked up. Out here on the plains it's windy like nowhere else I've ever been. Even when it seems calm, the wind can come up out of nowhere. Still one moment, then windier than all get-out the next. It was like that that morning, still. Chad was a doughy little fucker who thought he was hard 'cause of a short stint in juvie when he was fifteen, but he didn't have any experience roughing-in houses, so he was doomed to carrying lumber, stringing cords and air hoses, and fetching tools, cleaning up, whatever grunt work needed to be done. He was carrying plywood up the pitch above me for the other guys to nail down, and when he got close to the top, a wind came up. It blew over the top of the roof and caught the 4 x 8 sheet he was carrying. I was in the middle of a long cut, and out of the corner of my eye I saw him fighting it. I should have just taken my finger off the trigger, left the saw where it was, but I didn't. I was sure he had enough sense to just let go of the plywood, let the wind take it, but that was my mistake. The dumb sonofabitch hung on, I'll give him that, but damn if he didn't ride it out all the way down the roof and into me. It's amazing he didn't knock us both off. I don't know how, but in the collision, I managed to get the saw through the wood and, even with the guard working, into my left hand. The blade only bumped against the first knuckle of my index finger, and as I gathered myself up amidst the tangle of Chad's arms and legs, the plywood leaning against the top of the dormer above us, I thought maybe I'd gotten lucky and only nicked myself. You have those kinds of close calls all the time, so often that if you do the job long enough, they don't even really spook you anymore. I knew I'd gotten myself, but I'd hoped it wasn't bad—a few stitches, maybe. I pushed the plywood out of the way and looked at my left hand. It was like one of those brain teasers where there are two identical pictures, only in one there is some little difference. It's hard to find at first, but once you see it, you can't take your eyes off it. That's how it was for a split second before I realized my finger was gone. The blood didn't squirt like you see in the movies. A steady drip, more like. And it didn't hurt as bad as I would have imagined, either. Not yet.

"Shit, Coleman, you cut your finger off," Chad said nonchalantly when he sat up, as if it were something as minor as a stain on my shirt.

I wanted to beat his ass right then, but I had more important things to do, like find my finger.

"Give me your T-shirt," I said, and Chad looked at me like he couldn't figure out why I wanted it. "To wrap my fuckin' hand! C'mon, take it off!"

When I stepped toward Chad to take his shirt, I noticed out of the corner of my eye something rolling down the roof, and just when it went over the edge I recognized what it was—my finger. It must've been up against my boot, and when I moved, gravity took over. Once I'd wrapped Chad's shirt around my hand, I climbed as quickly down through the house as I could. Chad yelled behind me: "Hey! Coleman cut off his finger!"

A couple of the guys must've seen what happened or heard Chad yell because by the time I got out of the house, two of them, Doug and Rob, a couple real dipshits, were waiting for me. As I searched the ground for my finger, Doug, this punk kid who thought he knew everything, said, "What'd you do, Coleman, scratch yourself?" Since the bloodstained shirt around my hand apparently wasn't enough, I stepped to him and pulled the T-shirt back from my finger-stump. The color in his face drained, and he looked like he might pass out.

"Fuck, man, you really did it, didn't you?" Rob said. "We thought—Jesus, you got the whole fuckin' thing."

I rewrapped my hand. "You see my finger anywhere?"

Rob looked at me like I'd asked him some deep philosophical question. "Didn't think to look," he said.

Doug had stepped away to lean on a sawhorse, so Rob helped me take up the search. It had only been a few minutes, but the shock must've been wearing off because my hand was throbbing, though still not as bad as it would. The blood had soaked through the shirt and was dripping onto the ground. Cradling my hand to my chest, I looked all over. But the dirt and the sawdust and the scrap pieces of wood made for good finger-hiding.

At the time I wasn't even thinking about trying to find my finger so that it could be reattached; I just wanted to find it. It was *my* finger.

About that time, Steve came around the corner of the house and said, "What the hell you guys standing around fuckin' Shep for?"

"We're looking for Coleman's finger," Rob said, and then, as if that needed further explanation, "He cut it off."

"*Jesus,*" Steve said and came over to me. "Let me see." When I pulled back the blood-soaked T-shirt to show him, he said, "Shit yeah, you did. How'd—"

"Found it!" Rob looked almost giddy, like a kid who found the prize in a scavenger hunt. He brought my finger to me, holding it like a catsup-smeared French fry, before placing it in the palm of my right hand. It looked small, and it felt much lighter than I would have expected.

"All right," Steve said, sighing. "Let's get you to the hospital."

I didn't like the feel of carrying my severed digit, so I dropped it in the pocket of my shirt, figured that was as good a place as any.

The small hospital was just a little south of town, and we were there in less than ten minutes. Steve didn't say anything on the ride over, but he kept sighing and shaking his head. Somehow it made me feel like I'd disappointed him. He pulled his truck around the circle drive at the emergency room entrance and said, "This is as far as I go. Give me your keys, and I'll have one of the boys bring your truck by later." I handed him my keys. "You're a good worker, but . . ." he gestured to my bloody T-shirt–wrapped hand. He reached into his wallet and handed me a full week's pay though it was only Wednesday and said, "We're done here, okay."

"I know," I said and got out of his truck. I knew there was nothing he could do for me, and so I didn't expect anything else. All told, he was an all right boss.

Luckily there was no one else in the emergency room when I checked in, under a different name, so they got to me quickly. I could tell they didn't believe me when I told them I'd chopped off my finger building a birdhouse for my kid, but it wasn't any of their business how I'd managed it, only that I had. They asked where my finger was, and when I pulled it out of my pocket, the nurse almost laughed. "You should've had that on ice," she said as she put on rubber gloves and took my finger. I thought that was just something from bad hospital TV shows and I told her so. "You got here quickly enough, we might be able to save it."

Long story short, I'm now a nine-fingered man, not because I didn't keep my severed finger on ice, but because I don't have insurance. Since cutting off my finger wasn't "life threatening," and reattaching it was not considered "medically necessary" and therefore an "elective procedure," they wouldn't call in the orthopedic surgeon from Omaha to reattach it. Bullshit, but what was I supposed to do? The kicker? I don't even know where my finger is. I'm not sure what I would've done with it, but the sonofabitch was mine and I would've liked to have had a say in where it ended up.

The doctor had me on some pretty heavy-duty shit, and he probably shouldn't have released me under my own power, but I think the hospital was more than happy to get rid of a charity case like me.

Walking through the parking lot, I knew the drive back was going to be pretty hairy. If I turned my head, everything went blurry before slowly coming back into focus. I've driven drunk more times than I care to admit, but this was something in a class by itself. There weren't that many cars in the lot, so I found my truck easily enough. It was unlocked and the keys hung from the ignition—who's going to steal a rusted-out S-10 pickup? I hadn't really thought about how difficult driving was going to be until I started my truck. My hand was wrapped up like a boxing glove with only the tips of my remaining fingers poking out of the wrap. Normally, I'd steer with my left hand while I shifted with my right, but I couldn't really do that with my hand. Getting out of the parking lot wasn't easy; not only was I stoned on some premium medical-grade painkillers, I had to crank hard on the wheel with only my right hand to make the sharp turns. Once I was out on the road, I could balance the steering wheel with the tips of the three fingers of my left hand while I shifted with my right, but every time I touched the wheel a jolt of pain shot through my hand and up my arm. I was groggy, and everything felt the way it does when you're underwater. I took it slow to the Wahoo Pharmacy—the last thing I needed was to wreck my only means of getting out of this town—and I nosed up to the curb in front of the store.

The cowbell clanked above the door, announcing I'd come in, and I took my prescription straight to the back. The place smelled like a Band-Aid. The kid working the counter looked at me like I was some kind of zombie, which wasn't far off from how I felt. "Just a minute, sir," he said and walked to the back. I put my hand on the counter to steady the room. A woman in a white coat came from the back. "It'll be a few minutes, sir. If you'll just have a seat."

I staggered to the row of hard-backed plastic chairs against the wall. Everything still seemed in slow motion, but whatever they gave me at the hospital was wearing off. My scalp was tingling, and my hand started throbbing—really throbbing. It was finally feeling like I'd cut my finger off. Every heartbeat was like a hammer coming down on my hand, so I tried holding my breath to slow my pulse, but that only made it worse. I closed my eyes and tried thinking of something, anything, to keep my mind occupied, but nothing worked. The pain overwhelmed my thoughts. I started to sweat, and I couldn't stop squirming in my seat like some little kid with a case of ADD who'd gone off his meds.

Though I was coming down, I was still stoned enough to think I could actually hear the pain, so in my head I tried singing some song one of the rednecks on the crew had blasted over and over during lunch break a couple weeks ago. I didn't know the title—I don't pay attention to that stuff—or even much of the song, but a couple guys stood in the bed of a pickup caroling out a catchy part: *Bulldozers and dirt, bulldozers and dirt, behind the trailer my dessert, I don't mean no harm, I just like to flirt, but most of all I like bulldozers and dirt.* It had been stuck in my head ever since, and now I was more than happy to sing it to myself. On my third time through, it seemed to be working a bit to quiet the sound of my pain, but then the cowbell clanked and got me off track, and I couldn't get the song back.

I opened my eyes to the sound of flip-flops slapping the bottom of someone's feet. A small town like this one, I half expected it to be some pigtailed little girl coming in to buy candy or something, but the woman who appeared at the mouth of the aisle in cutoff jean shorts and a white tank top was no little girl. I didn't know her name, but I recognized her from the Stardust up the road in Colon. She was blond and thin, too thin if you ask me, but in a place like the Stardust she was something to look at. I saw her a few times with the same guy, but she was always a flirt and a lush, making the local old-timers uncomfortable with the way she moved on the dance floor. I'd tipped a longneck her way a few times and got a wink or two in return. Thought of asking her to dance once or twice—there was only old danceable country music on the juke—but she had a wild look about her, and I never got deep enough into the bottle to do it.

At the counter the kid asked if he could help her, gesturing to the prescription slip she clutched tightly in her hand. "I want to talk to Marcy," she said, and when he told her he could take the prescription to Ms. Miller, she replied, "Goddamn it, just get Marcy." After the kid went to the back, she jutted out her hip, put her hands flat on the counter, and looked over in my direction. I nodded at her, thinking she might recognize me, but it was as if she didn't even see me.

This woman provided some distraction from the pain, but it was steadily creeping up my arm, past my elbow now, so when the kid came back to tell the woman Marcy would be right with her, I blurted out: "Hey, man, how long's it take to count out some friggin' pills?"

"We're working on it, sir," the kid said. I wondered if they were trying to check me out, if they were running the name I'd given the hospital, or if that was even something they were capable of doing.

When the pharmacist came back out, I pushed myself up in my chair, but before I could stand, she said to me, "I'll be right with you." I slumped back down, mumbling something about being there first. It might have just been the drugs making me paranoid, but I was seriously worried that they were somehow onto me and just stalling until the cops came.

In the meantime, the woman and the pharmacist had both leaned their heads close together. "I didn't get word," the pharmacist said, barely loud enough for me to hear. "It's a week early."

"I know, but Tommy, he said to just tell you he'd sent me. Said a week early wouldn't matter."

"I gotta—"

"C'mon, Marcy."

"Let me call Tommy and—"

"Marcy, I need this," the woman said. "Bad. I'll clear it with Tommy. Please."

I'm no expert, but it looked like she was trying to screw somebody out of something. It didn't much matter to me as long as I got mine.

"Even if I could, I can't. I don't have enough yet," the pharmacist said.

The woman pushed herself away from the counter. "Fuck you, Marcy." She turned and looked at me, this time like she actually saw me, before stomping down the aisle and out the door, the cowbell clanking after her.

The kid came from the back and handed the pharmacist a large bottle, a tube of ointment, and a box of sterile bandages. She motioned for me, and when I stood, whatever I was on had worn off enough that the floor didn't swing out from under me, but my whole arm felt like death.

The pharmacist was short with me and only gave the basics: change the dressing twice a day, apply the ointment, and take the Percocet with food and only as needed, but don't drink or operate any vehicles or machinery. I nodded along with her instructions, paid, and left.

So there I was sitting in my truck, out of a job, my hand bandaged up like a boxing glove, less one finger than I'd rolled into this silly-named town with. And, to top it all off, I couldn't even get the goddamn bottle of pills opened with only one hand. I had it squeezed between my knees, fighting like hell to get the lid off. I was on the verge of smashing it against the steering wheel or getting out and stomping on it, when someone said, "Need some help with that?"

"*Fuck!*" I said and nearly jumped out of my seat, the pill bottle clattering to the floorboard. I felt like I'd been caught with my dick in my hand. My heart was pounding, which made my hand throb harder. When I looked up, I saw it was the woman who'd come into the pharmacy. "Jesus. You scared the piss out of me."

"Just saw you were having some troubles. Thought I'd see if I could help."

A light breeze kicked up and carried the overly sweet smell of her perfume into the cab of my truck. It was fruity, like something a high school girl wears. I'd never seen her this close before. Outside of the forgiving glow of bar lighting, I could see her blond was from a bottle, and where I'd pegged her as early thirties, now I wasn't so sure. She had the deep lines around her mouth and at the corners of her eyes that come from forced smiles during unkind times. It was obvious up close that she was pretty once; it was there, but you had to look hard.

"Name's Jolene," she said and stuck her hand though the open window.

I reached across my body and took her hand. It was soft and moist, but my hand came away dry. "Jolene? Like that old country song?"

"Sure, sweetie."

"Ray," I said, though it was as much my real name as Jolene was hers. I didn't know where this was going, and after what I'd seen her try to pull in the pharmacy, my real name wasn't any of her business.

"What happened to your hand?" She crossed her arms and rested them on my door. Her breasts were small, but with the way she was leaning forward, I saw quite a bit of her black bra and the faded blue smudge of a tattoo looking like it was trying to climb out.

I spared her the whole story and just told her I'd cut my finger off at work. If I'd been looking for sympathy, Jolene was the wrong place. She didn't seem bothered at all by what I told her. She said matter-of-factly, "So, need some help?"

Before I could answer, she opened my door and, laying her head directly in my lap, reached under the pedals where the pill bottle had settled. Those slippery hands must've made it hard for her to grab the bottle because she was down there quite a while.

"Found it," she said as she came up, and she smiled as I adjusted myself. She twisted off the cap, fished out a pill, and held it in her palm. "Here."

I took the pill and placed it between my teeth and grabbed an old bottle of water that was on the bench seat. After I swallowed the pill, I looked at her. She was smiling at me in a way I'd seen plenty of times before. She wanted something. My pills, most likely. "Take one if you want. I got the whole bottle."

"Maybe later," she said and looked over the top of the cab. "Look, you're probably going to need some help tonight, right?" She looked back at me. "I mean, how's a man supposed to wash himself with one hand, let alone take care of his other needs?"

Though I'd never paid for it in a strict sense, I'd been with a couple women where a kind of unspoken arrangement was in place—they needed something: a place to crash for a weekend, a ride out of town, help moving out of their ex's, some work on their house, whatever—where it probably would have just been easier to have paid them outright. So even in my condition, I was under no illusion about what Jolene was getting at. She'd just had her head buried in my crotch, after all. I didn't know what she wanted in return for her help, but at that moment I wasn't opposed to letting the line out a little.

"You can drive," I said as I slid across the seat, careful to keep my hand elevated.

She chuckled when I told her where I was staying. "So that's where this is happening?"

"I don't know what's happening, but that's where I'm staying." I wasn't too worried about her knowing; I was paid through the end of the week at the Big Chief, and after that, I was gone.

She looked at me across the cab, as if surveying some kind of damage, and for just a moment her face relaxed into what I think was a real smile. But it was gone as quickly as it came.

The sun was setting when we pulled into the Big Chief. I told her which unit was mine, and she parked in front. I got out of the truck without bumping my hand on anything, but at my door I realized my room key was in my left front pocket. I started to reach in with my right hand, but Jolene stopped me. "See, that's what I'm here for," she said and plunged her hand far past the key in my pocket. The way her hand roamed around you'd think she didn't know what a key felt like. I braced myself against the door-jamb with my right hand and let Jolene do her thing. As I stood enjoying her search, I happened to look over at my neighbor, some old-timer sitting in a green-and-yellow aluminum folding chair in front of his open door, the light from the thirteen-inch TV flick-ering behind him. He raised his paper bag–wrapped bottle and showed me a few of his remaining teeth.

"Mind your business, old man," Jolene said when she saw he was looking. She took the key from my pocket, and the old man let out a wheezing "hee-heee."

Inside, Jolene took a quick look around the room and walked past the bed to the bathroom at the back and closed the door. The pipes groaned, and I heard the water running in the tub. I didn't know what to do, so I turned the knob of the ancient TV. One of those '90s sitcoms played across the screen. I kept the volume low and sat on the edge of the bed and watched the beautiful young people joke their way through their weekly crisis in their oversized New York City apartment. "You got anything to drink?" Jolene called over the noise of the water in the bathroom.

I took my bottle of Wild Turkey from the dresser drawer below the TV. I didn't have any cups, but Jolene didn't seem to be a woman who needed that kind of luxury. I tapped on the hollow-core door with the toe of my boot. The water stopped running, and she said, "C'mon in." I pushed open the door, and through the steam I saw Jolene lying back in the tub, her hair piled atop her head, her nip-ples poking out of the water. The blue smudge I saw earlier was a faded rose, its stem extending down and curling under the inside of her left breast. The water distorted the darkness of her closely trimmed pubic hair.

"You gonna just stand there? Told you I was gonna help you get clean."

I wasn't sure how this was going to work, the bathroom was barely big enough for one person to turn around in, but at that point I was more than willing to give it a shot. I sat on her clothes piled on the toilet seat and put the bottle on the floor by the tub. I started untying my boots, but with one hand it was slow going. "Here," Jolene said and leaned over the edge of the tub. She got my boots off and then told me to stand so she could work on my belt and the front of my pants. I got my shirt off and stood there naked. I'd put in almost a full day's work, and the smell of dirt and sawdust and sweat filled the tiny space. I raised my arm and made as if to sniff my armpit. "Damn, I'm ripe."

"Well, get in here, then."

There wasn't really room for two, and it wasn't easy lowering myself into the water with only one hand. We were tangled and uncomfortable facing each other, so Jolene got behind me. It was still a tight fit, and plenty of water slopped out of the tub, but she seemed willing to make it work and I wasn't going to argue.

She took her time getting me clean, us passing the bottle back and forth, and it wasn't long before I'd settled back against her. I hadn't soaked in a tub like this in a long time. Jolene was working an angle, I knew, and I wanted to confront her, ask her outright what she wanted before I got myself into something, but it felt so good in the water, I decided to let those thoughts go, just for a while. It didn't hurt that the booze and the Percocet were doing their voodoo on me.

After we'd been in the water long enough for my toes to get pruney, she asked, "How's your hand?"

I had my left elbow resting on the edge of the tub, my hand pointing straight up. "Still throbbing some."

"Another pill?"

I nodded, probably against my better judgment, and she got out of the tub, dripping water on the curling linoleum. I looked over my shoulder and watched her ass waggle as she left the bathroom. I heard the pill bottle rattle in the other room, and when she came back in and put the pill between my lips, I had a fleeting thought that she was trying to get me fucked up enough that she could rob me. She had to've figured if I was staying at the Big Chief, I probably didn't have a bank account in town, so there had to be cash in the room. There was, though not as much as she might've thought. I'd worked out a deal with a cousin of mine in Kansas City; I wired most of my cash to him and he held it for me.

But all that didn't stop me from swallowing the pill with the whiskey she put to my lips.

"And one for Mama," she said, and I saw she had a pill between her teeth. She took a drink and it was gone. "I think you're clean enough." She offered me a hand to help me out of the tub. "Let's go."

After drying me off, she took the bottle and my good hand, led me into the other room, and sat me on the unmade bed. She pushed my chest back, and as she straddled me, I saw her look around the room. The Big Chief didn't have a cleaning staff, so the room wasn't near clean, but I always keep my shit organized and in my bag so I can get the hell out of Dodge quickly if I need to. I wondered if she was scouting the room, trying to find where I might keep my money. The bit of cash I kept here wasn't anywhere she'd find.

She started to grind on me, but with the combination of the pills and booze, nothing was happening. It felt good, sure, but I couldn't concentrate. That didn't seem to keep her from trying, though. She had the porno-thing down, with the moaning and the lip biting and the hair swinging. I knew that there wasn't much time; the second pill was beginning to work. Everything at the edge of my vision was turning murky, and I could feel myself losing control. It was only a matter of time before I was too fucked up to keep Jolene from doing whatever it was she was going to do.

I grabbed her hip with my right hand to slow her down. "So, what do you want?"

"I want you to fuck me," she said, and the way she had her hands in her hair and was swinging her head around was starting to freak me out.

"No," I said and squeezed her hip tighter. "For this. It can't just be the pills."

She swung her head forward and pushed her hands hard against my chest. "You think I'm some kind of fuckin' whore?"

"Not any more than me. Or anyone else out there." I looked at her above me, but focusing was becoming a problem. "So?" She looked off toward the door. "Just the pills?"

"I don't want any more of your fucking pills. If that was all I wanted, I would've had them already. Besides, asshole, *you* need them."

"But at the pharmacy—"

"You don't know anything. That was—Jesus, forget it."

"So it's money?"

"God," she said and slumped over onto the bed next to me. "Of course it's money. It's *always* money. You should know that. But you don't have enough, and—I'm fucked."

I didn't know how much she needed, but however much it was, it wasn't worth a night of sex—if I could even get it up—and I wasn't interested in charity.

"Okay," she said and pushed her hair back from her forehead. "I got pulled over. A fucking broken taillight, but when the cop ran my license it must've come up that I was on paper, so he asked to search the car. Sure, got nothing to hide, I said. Besides, it was my mom's van. 'Course I didn't know she had an unregistered .38 stashed under the front seat from before, when one of her old men had made some threats. Been there so long she'd forgotten about it. Now I got a court date in a couple days, and it's real this time. I'm looking at five *years*."

"Shit," I said. She *was* fucked. And, considering the circumstances and what she'd tried to pull at the pharmacy, she was desperate. I should have left it at that, but I had to ask. "What's the money for?"

"What money?" She looked at me.

"The money you said you need. If you're going away, why do you need it?"

"My kids. They're going to live with my mom in Council Bluffs, but her disability money, it isn't enough."

I'd be lying if I said I didn't feel bad for her, but *her* kids weren't *my* problem. "Look," I said, "I'd like to help you and all, but—"

"I told you I don't want your money."

"Then what's all this?" I said and nodded my head at her naked body.

"I need a favor."

"If it's got anything to do with that shit at the pharmacy, I'm out."

"No. That's on me. I just need to buy some time."

"I sold out yesterday," I said and laughed, and I knew I was completely stoned because I'm not usually that quick.

"What?"

"Huh?" I said, still laughing.

"I need a few more days before my court date to get some more money together."

"So," I said, calming down. "What's that got to do with me?"

"I want you to stab me."

"*What*? You want me to—are you fucking nuts?"

"I'm in the hospital a couple two, three days, my date gets postponed."

She climbed out of bed and went to her purse. My mind lurched and stumbled as I tried to make sense of it all. I squeezed my eyes shut, and when I opened them, she was on my lap again and in her hand was a comically large pocketknife. Closed, it was easily seven or eight inches. It was a knife made to be engraved and displayed.

"It's my son's. He won it at the carnival."

"I know you're in a bind, but this is—I can't stab you."

"Just in the leg, or here in my side. But deep enough to lay me up."

"Nah, you gotta go. I can't," I said and arched my back so she would let me up.

"I'm not going anywhere. You're doing this." She looked right at me, right into my eyes, and I realized that was the first time we'd made real eye contact all night.

"The fuck I am," I said and shoved her off me. "Get your ass outta here."

"No! I *can't*—look," she said. "Do it, or I tell Tommy you put me up to that shit at the pharmacy."

I didn't know who Tommy was, and it took me a second to realize what she meant. "The fuck I care about Tommy?"

"Oh boy, you *better*."

I had a hard time believing anyone with the name Tommy was that dangerous, especially in Wahoo, Nebraska.

"And all I gotta do is say you made me try to steal his shit. He knows I'd never pull anything like that."

"Except you did."

She rolled off the side of the bed, went to her purse, and pulled out her cell phone. "Do it, or I'll call him right-fuckin'-now. Don't believe me, just see what happens."

I had options: I could call her bluff and wait and see, or I could pack my shit and leave. I was on the road in a couple days anyway, but the last thing I needed was some drug dealer, small-time or not, looking for me. I honestly didn't think I was in any real danger, but I didn't want to be looking over my shoulder for the next few weeks, either. Or I could just do what she wanted, as fucked as it was, and then blow.

"Give me the knife," I said. It was bat-shit crazy, and I just wanted to be done with it.

She kept her cell phone in her hand and brought the knife to me. We traded places on the bed. I couldn't open the blade with one hand, so she opened it for me. The blade was shiny, but it didn't look very sharp; it was more novelty than knife. "So how're we doing this?"

"I don't know. I don't want to watch." She sat up on her knees, pushed her hair back, and took a deep breath. "I'll close my eyes and you just do it."

I weighed the knife in my hand and took a few practice jabbing motions. I'd never stabbed anyone before, and besides, I was using my off-hand. And the drugs didn't help. "Where do you want it?"

She shook her head. "Just do it."

I stood before her, still naked—we both were—and searched her body for the right spot. The longer I stood there, the more the weirdness of the situation settled in.

"C'mon, goddammit, just do it!" she yelled at me, and when she did, I thrust the knife into the spot I happened to be looking at—her upper leg, where her thigh met her hip. The knife kind of bounced off; the tip broke the skin, but only just barely. She let out a guttural scream from somewhere deep inside. "*Mother*fuck!" Then she flipped out and started swinging at me. I turned and raised my right shoulder to try to deflect some of her blows, but one of them glanced off and hit my left hand. Even with the pills, white starbursts lit up behind my eyelids, and before I could even catch my breath enough to yell out, I'd plunged the knife into the fleshy side of her stomach. Her eyes went wide and her face drained of all the tightness, and strangely, she looked disturbingly younger. The noise she made was less a scream than a whining moan. This time the knife didn't bounce off, and I had to pull it from her. My stomach turned and I heaved, vomiting whiskey and bile onto the floor. She grabbed where I stabbed her and fell back onto the bed, curling her legs to her body. Blood poured from between her fingers and ran down her stomach, pooling on the mattress. She squirmed around, spreading blood all over the bedsheets, making noises I didn't know a human could make in between her *Oh God, Oh God*s.

I took a step back and stared at her. Then the adrenaline kicked in, and I stumbled over the corner of the bed and reached down to the baseboard where I had my money stashed and pulled the cut piece of wood away from the wall. The angle was awkward with my right hand, but I dug the roll of money out of the hole. I tore off five or six bills and tossed them on the bed and grabbed Jolene's cell phone. I saw the terror in her eyes as I pried it from her grip.

In the bathroom, I collected my clothes and shoved them with the rest of my stuff in my bag. After awkwardly stepping into my boots, I grabbed the knife off the floor where I'd dropped it. I wiped the blade on the comforter and put the knife in my bag. I grabbed the bottle of pills off the TV stand and slung my bag over my shoulder and opened the front door. My neighbor was gone and the parking lot was clear. I ran, naked, to my truck and tossed my bag into the cab. I got it started and in gear before I dialed 911. I told the dispatcher that I'd heard screaming coming from a unit in the Big Chief. When she asked my name, I ended the call and smashed the back of the phone against the shift knob until the battery came out.

I pulled out of the lot as calmly as possible and hit Highway 77 south. I wasn't too worried about being naked; it was dark, and as long as I didn't get pulled over, it wouldn't be a problem. I thought I heard sirens in the distance, but I couldn't be sure. Though the adrenaline had sobered me up considerably, it wasn't easy keeping the truck between the lines. I had to keep squeezing my eyes closed and opening them so my vision stayed clear. As I drove, the ambient light of Omaha reflected off the clouds, lighting the eastern edge of the sky. I thought about my fingerprints in the room, if I'd been seen driving away, and what Jolene would tell the cops—if they got there in time.

I got off 77 before Lincoln, cut through Waverly, and stuck to county roads, jogging east toward Highway 67 and then south. After I'd driven for close to an hour, passing only a handful of cars, I pulled onto the shoulder of the highway where it passed over Weeping Water Creek. In just the dome light, I struggled getting on my jeans in the small cab of the truck, and though I couldn't get them buttoned, at least I wasn't naked anymore. Putting on a shirt was a little easier. Dressed, I took the knife and Jolene's cell phone and battery and stood at the rail of the bridge. Weeping Water was more a wet, tree-lined gulch gouged between two cornfields than an actual creek, but it would do. I chucked all three off the bridge as best I could with my right hand. I couldn't see, but I heard them splash in the water.

I continued south through the rolling hills into Kansas. I made Topeka by midnight, and I didn't look back once.

HOME SHOPPING

Darlene and Eddie know, as soon as the realtor turns onto the tree-lined, brick-paved street, that the house on the corner will be the one. It has to be; it's the third and final house of the day.

The realtor, Maxine, pulls into the driveway of the renovated Victorian. The house is white, but all the trim and spindles and cornices are painted in a pattern of muted gray, blue, and green. A large swing hangs on the wraparound porch, and the yard is perfectly manicured with a Bradford pear just to the side of the house. "I know you'll love this property; it's simply perfect," Maxine says over her shoulder to Darlene and Eddie, searching in her bag on the passenger seat for the folder with the listing. "It's got five bedrooms—plenty of room for the kids—three baths, and all new amenities. I know it's on the top end of your budget, but . . . you've just *got* to see it."

Darlene leans across Eddie's lap to look up at the house. This close, Eddie's cologne is too strong. It smells piney and cheap, much too old-smelling for a man in his mid-twenties. His pants are wrinkled, too; the rest of his clothing, a dark green polo and lightweight brown sport coat, looks fine, but she can't believe she didn't notice his pants earlier. She quickly checks her own outfit, charcoal slacks and a white blouse, to see that everything is in place and then looks out the window at the house. It's big and old and exactly the kind of house Darlene had always dreamed of living in. She and Eddie had worked a few big houses before, but never one so nice. She knows the people who live in these kinds of houses have to have money, so there is a good chance they'll find what they're looking for.

Pulling back from the window, Darlene looks at Eddie. His face is pale, and his eyes—only a little bloodshot, like maybe he's tired—dart around in their sockets. He's fighting it, but she can tell. He rubs the side of his nose with the back of his hand and then pushes up his sleeve and scratches his forearm, digging his fingernails into his skin, leaving it blotchy and red. This is new. Darlene reaches across and holds Eddie's arm.

"Maxine, can we have just a moment alone to discuss the last house?" Darlene asks.

"Absolutely! Take as much time as you need. I'll go unlock the door."

"Great, thanks," Darlene says and smiles. She watches Maxine walk away from the car, her wide hips swaying beneath the tight blue business suit, her permed hair stiff in the breeze. When she is far enough away, Darlene turns and glares at Eddie. "What the hell is this?"

"What?" he says and sniffs. "I'm fine. Let's just do this and get it over with."

"You don't look fine. What's with the scratching?"

"I'm fine—or no worse off than you," he says and nods down at her hands. "Let's go in and hope for the best."

Darlene looks at her hands. They're shaking. It's only barely visible, but still. She hadn't even noticed. She opens and closes her hands, making tight fists and releasing them. When did it get like this?

"You ready?" Eddie asks, looking directly at Darlene.

She takes a deep breath and closes her eyes as she exhales. She opens her eyes and looks at her hands resting quietly on her lap. "Ready."

When they get out of the car, there is a touch of honeysuckle in the warm summer air. As they approach the house, Darlene is even more impressed. Maxine is right; this house is perfect. For a moment, forgetting why they're there, Darlene sees herself sitting on the porch swing, drinking a tall glass of iced tea, a book open on her lap, and two children playing in the yard. Her reverie is broken when Eddie whistles softly and says loud enough for the realtor to hear: "Quite a house."

On the front porch Maxine hands them the listing. "Take a quick look at that, and we'll head on in."

"Look, honey," Darlene says and points at the listing. "It's got a rec room—the kids'll love that—and a den off the family room that we could turn into an office for you." They've been doing this now off and on for nearly a year, and they've gotten good at it, but it still surprises Darlene how easy it is. The small realty companies typically did less checking, so all they have to do is tell the realtor they're thinking of moving to the area in the next few months, but they want to get the lay of the land and the housing market first. All that's left is to dress up and invent a story about who they are, and generally the realtors buy it. Her favorite part is making up the stories. They usually go by Kristen and Brent, and sometimes they are newlyweds, just back from honeymooning in Hawaii, looking to put a large down payment on a house with their wedding money, but most of the time she's a housewife with two children, both boys, and Eddie works as a young, hotshot investment banker or an architect; it doesn't really matter as long as she can play the loving stay-at-home mom.

"Shall we?" Maxine asks, and Darlene looks again at Eddie and raises her eyebrows. If he can't pull off his part, there's no way she can do what they both need her to do.

"Sure, but I can tell Kristen's already fallen in love with it," Eddie says and lightly squeezes Darlene's elbow the way Brent might.

Darlene lets out a deep breath and smiles. "Okay, I can't wait any longer. I *must* see inside this house," she says in the way she knows Kristen would.

Though she and Eddie are there for one reason, they can't rush it. They have to wait for just the right moment and be ready when it comes. Lately Eddie has been careless and forcing it, intentionally trying to draw the realtors away, but that's sloppy and dangerous. Earlier at the first house, Eddie pushed too hard to see the basement while Darlene was checking out the family room. Maxine had called out to Darlene to come with her and Eddie to see the basement. "You'll love the bonus room," she'd said. Darlene had no choice but to follow. She was sure Maxine hadn't suspected anything, but Eddie should've known better.

At the front door, just before Eddie steps inside, Darlene holds the sleeve of his sport coat. "Relax," she mouths when he looks at her. She sees the muscles in his jaw flex as his eyes, shifty before, now pierce directly into her and stop her where she stands. Then Eddie pulls his arm away from Darlene and steps inside as Maxine describes the flooring in the entryway. The cool, conditioned air hits Darlene in the face, filling the void left by Eddie. She stands on the doorstep, frozen by Eddie's look. They used to have fun doing this. They even had a name for it: *home shopping*. After a day of home shopping, they'd barely be able to get in their apartment before they were tearing at each other's clothes. The rush of the day would finally reach a head, and it would boil over into their lovemaking. Sometimes, they wouldn't even be able to make it home, and they'd pull off somewhere and frantically go at it in the car. Later, they'd lie in bed and build their dream home from the parts they liked of each house, or they'd describe to one another what it would be like to live in one of them. Even then Darlene knew it was just a fantasy, but at least they had that. But now? That look, and the shaking in the car? Things were changing, or had changed, without her even realizing it.

If possible, the inside of the house is even nicer than the outside. The hardwood floors have been redone, the walls have all been painted neutral colors, and the decorating is sparse, yet tasteful, lived-in: all this without sacrificing the home's character. Maxine leads them through the front of the house, first the sitting room and living room, which she points out is wired for surround sound, and then the dining room, toward the back and into the kitchen, where the smell of freshly baked cookies lingers in the air. Darlene smiles until she sees an air freshener plugged in an outlet above the counter. While Maxine describes to Eddie the high-quality materials used on the kitchen remodel, Darlene watches as he opens some of the cabinets, running his thumb along the mitered joints and lifting up and down slightly to check the strength of the hinges, as if inspecting for himself firsthand the craftsmanship. From where she's standing she can see what's inside when Eddie opens each cabinet. Nothing, or at least nothing that concerns the two of them. But it's impressive to watch how convincing he is, and for a moment Darlene regrets thinking he was getting careless. The shiftiness is gone from his eyes and his movements are fluid; there isn't a trace of what he was doing in the car only a few minutes before.

While Eddie asks more questions about the kitchen, something about how to maintain the granite countertops, Darlene notices the collage of colorful child drawings and A+ papers, business card magnets and menus, snapshots, announcements, and to-do lists stuck to the front of the stainless steel refrigerator. One of the pictures is of a family, presumably the one living in the house, the parents and two kids, a boy and a girl, standing at the base of a mountain, bundled in their snowsuits, holding their skis and poles, red-faced and smiling. The wife, who Darlene thinks can't be but a few years older than she is, is beautiful, and even in the bulky snowsuit, it's clear she still has her figure, and the husband has the rugged features she always thinks of as fireman-like, yet he looks sophisticated, even after a day of skiing. Both kids appear happy and healthy, poster children for the perfect American family. This is it, Darlene thinks as she looks at the accumulation of a life stuck on the refrigerator, and she feels a slight tightening at the back of her throat. When the realtor asks if they would like to see the sun porch and backyard, Darlene swallows hard and says, "Of *course.*"

On the way out of the kitchen, Maxine shows Darlene the walk-in pantry. She steps inside and looks at the shelves of cereal, canned foods, boxed pasta dinners, and spices on one side, and seemingly every known cooking contraption on the other. "With two growing boys, I'll bet it wouldn't take long to fill this up!" Maxine says, and Darlene smiles and gives her a practiced knowing look, as if to say, "You don't know the half of it."

Next to the pantry is a small breakfast nook that opens to the sun porch overlooking the large backyard. Oversized wicker furniture is organized around a glass-topped table, and Darlene can see herself with the husband from the picture, sitting out here drinking a cup of coffee on some Sunday morning, or entertaining guests that have migrated outside for drinks or to smoke after a dinner party. It's easy enough to imagine, and if she tries hard, she can even see herself with Eddie doing those same things. But Darlene knows it's only make-believe and isn't helping anything. Maybe she's the one that's slipping, not Eddie. When they first started, she was nervous and it was all about the take, but now that that part is easier, it's harder not to get caught up in the fantasy. She needs to clear her head and make the move. "I'm sorry, but I really need to use the bathroom. Would it be okay, or do you think the homeowners would mind?"

Maxine hesitates a moment, then smiles. "I don't think they'd mind. After all, if you gotta go, you gotta go, right?" she says and forces a realtor laugh. Then she leans in as if to whisper. "We'll tell them you were testing the facilities." Maxine steps back and laughs again, and behind her Eddie is smiling and nodding. "There's a bathroom just off the living room."

Eddie takes advantage of the situation. "The listing says there's a workshop out back. Do you think we could check it out while we're waiting?" Darlene and Eddie had found that for every realtor who wouldn't let them separate, there were a half dozen who, if they thought they were going to make a sale, would let them do pretty much whatever they wanted.

"You do woodworking?" Maxine asks, and Darlene thinks she seems a bit unsure.

"I like to tinker," Eddie says. "It helps me clear my head after a long day at the office."

"Oh," Maxine says. "Well, you're going to love the shed. It's wired for electricity, so it's all ready to go. Darlene, you can join us out back when you're through."

Darlene knows Eddie is good at this part and can buy her upward of ten minutes, so she doesn't hurry though the house. She takes time to look at the details she missed on the way in. On the mantel in the living room are the two kids' school portraits and the couple's wedding photo, and though it has to be close to ten years old based on the kids, it doesn't look dated like most wedding photos. Both the husband and the wife look stylish standing before the ornate altar. Darlene wonders if she and Eddie will ever have a picture like this one. There was a time when she believed they would, but as hard as she tries now, she can't imagine it.

She runs her hand over the bulky newel post and up the smooth railing, and the oak treads creak slightly under her feet as she climbs the stairs to the second floor. She passes a bathroom at the top of the stairs and only peeks in the two kids' rooms. There's something about snooping in a child's room that Darlene can't abide; if they were teenagers, maybe, but these kids are too young. The master bedroom is at the end of the hall. The room is large, and it's obvious the couple spent a lot of money remodeling it. There is crown molding on the ceiling, and her feet sink into the new plush carpet. It probably wasn't an en suite originally, but the couple has added a bathroom in the corner of the room.

Darlene walks around the bed and stops at the dresser. The top is cleared off for the showing, but she knows that in one of the drawers she'll find jewelry. Not the good stuff, she's sure that's locked away, but the pieces the woman wears most often. Just to satisfy her curiosity, Darlene opens each drawer until she finds a small box in the bottom one. Inside are two pairs of earrings, a watch, and a necklace. Nothing too fancy, but there they are. Though it would be easy, she doesn't risk taking valuables. People tend to notice when jewelry or cameras turn up missing, and besides, sometimes that stuff is hard to sell. She closes the box and pushes the drawer shut.

Darlene peeks out one of the bedroom windows down into the backyard and sees that Maxine is just now opening the shed for Eddie. In the large, open bathroom, Darlene looks at herself in the double glass doors of the medicine cabinet. She's come to learn that you never can tell which houses will have the good stuff and which ones won't, so it's always a mystery just before she opens the doors. It's a rush, not unlike swallowing a couple of the pills she finds. But this house, or her reaction to it, is different. She wonders if it's what she saw on the refrigerator or the house itself, but she knows better. She's seen pictures like that in houses all over, and she thinks, too, that the picture probably wouldn't have affected her if she'd had something in her system; and the house *is* perfect, everything she's ever wanted and more, but it's not as if they haven't been in nice houses before, she tells herself, and she tries hard to believe it. No, she thinks, it's the shaky hands in the car and

Eddie's scratching and digging at his arms and the look he gave her. All of it. Everything.

She knows what she needs to do, what Eddie expects, but now, here, she doesn't want to look because she's afraid of what's likely behind the doors. Instead, she opens each drawer in the vanity first, knowing she won't find any prescriptions. The last drawer she opens contains the woman's makeup. Darlene digs out a tube of lipstick, takes off the cap, and turns the bottom; the dark burgundy—called merlot—rises out of the tube, and she can see where the woman's lips last touched it. Looking in the mirror, she applies it. The color is too dark or her skin is too fair; it clashes with the freckles across her nose, but it feels nice on her lips.

She sets the lipstick on the counter, and she closes her eyes and takes a deep breath before opening the cabinet. Though she and Eddie need something, anything, she hopes all she'll find is Advil, cold medicine, and birth control pills.

Darlene places her purse on the vanity top and opens the cabinet, her reflection sliding off the mirror. Directly in the center of the cabinet, label facing out, sits a bottle of Xanax. "Goddamn it," Darlene says aloud and shakes her head and begins to cry softly. For a second she considers closing the cabinet and later, when Eddie asks, telling him they were clean. But she takes the bottle and opens it. It's about half full, so she can risk taking a small handful. Perfect. She puts the bottle back exactly the way it was and drops the pills in her purse. She scavenges the rest of the cabinet. Behind the Xanax is a full bottle of Valium, prescribed from a different doctor, from which she takes five or six pills, and stacked on the middle shelf are twelve or fifteen sample packs of Ambien CR. Darlene takes four, and then goes back for two more. She has to put one of her knees up on the counter to get to the top shelf, and when she does she's rewarded for her hard work. In the left-hand corner, behind two extra toothbrushes, some alcohol swabs, and a box of Band-Aids, are two bottles: one of OxyContin and the other of Percocet. "Jesus Christ," she says, both ashamed of the homeowners and surprised at her find. The OxyContin and the Percocet are dated from three years ago, and upon shaking the bottles, she guesses each is more than half full. Since they were far back in the corner, she breaks their rule of taking whole bottles and drops them in her purse. Closing the cabinet, she avoids looking at herself in the mirror. When she and Eddie first started doing this, it had been fun and sexy, something she was doing before it was time for her to be a grown-up, but now here she is almost twenty-five, crying in a stranger's bathroom with more pills in her purse than she'd ever taken before, and she isn't sure how or when it got this way.

When Darlene hears footsteps on the deck below, she grabs her purse and runs as lightly as she can through the bedroom and down the hall. She takes the stairs by twos and the bottles of OxyContin and Percocet rattle in her purse. She makes it to the bottom just as she hears the back door closing and Eddie's and Maxine's voices in the kitchen. She does her best to look calm, but she's breathing heavily and her heart is pounding so hard she's afraid they'll see it through her blouse.

"How's the workshop?" she asks as Maxine and Eddie enter the room, hoping to steer the conversation.

"Actually, it's really great," Eddie says, and Darlene notices his tone is different. "I'd finally have a space for all the projects I'd like to do." Darlene looks at Eddie and can tell by the way he's looking at her that something is wrong.

Maxine's overly sculpted eyebrows bunch together. "Are you all right, Kristen?"

"Sure," Darlene says, trying to act nonchalant. "Why?"

"Your eyes are puffy," Maxine says.

Darlene looks at Maxine, then at Eddie. "I think they must have a cat or something. I'm allergic. To cats." She sniffs and squints and rubs her eyes.

Maxine flips through several sheets of paper on her small clipboard. "I don't have anything in my notes about pets," she pauses, and Darlene and Eddie share another look. Darlene can see his eyes go to her lips. She'd forgotten about the lipstick. "But that doesn't mean they don't have any, just that there aren't any in the house right *now*. You poor thing. My son, bless his little heart, gets just like you do if he gets anywhere *near* a cat."

"Isn't it awful? And I just *love* cats." Darlene makes her voice as eager as she can.

"So does Henry," Maxine says and laughs, shaking her head sympathetically. Then she reaches into her purse, pulls out her cell phone, and opens her pictures. "Henry," she says and points at what looks to be a recent family photo.

"Good-lookin' kid," Eddie says over Maxine's shoulder.

"Oh, he's going to be a heartbreaker. Handsome, just like his father," Darlene says, leaning over Maxine's phone.

"Too handsome for his own good, if you ask me," Maxine says and shuts down her phone. For just a moment, Darlene sees the real Maxine, or at least a different Maxine, and she feels sorry for what she and Eddie are doing. Then Maxine pushes her shoulders back and says, "How about we take a quick look at the upstairs and get you outside for some fresh air?"

"That sounds wonderful."

Maxine starts up the stairs, but before following her, Eddie pauses and raises his eyebrows and Darlene nods her head slightly. Now is not the time. "I love the woodwork here on the stairs," Eddie says as he climbs, Darlene behind him squeezing her purse under her arm to keep the pill bottles quiet.

Maxine quickly shows them the upstairs, pausing in the hall-way only to tell them about the newly remodeled hall bath, and the closet space in both kids' rooms. In the master bedroom she takes a little more time to point out the details: the crown molding, the carpet, and the walk-in closet. Maxine then leads them into the master bathroom, and while she doesn't seem to notice that the light is on, Darlene sees her spot the lipstick standing near the edge of the counter. Maxine pauses before turning to Darlene.

They share a look and Darlene knows Maxine knows she used the lipstick, but Maxine doesn't say anything, and with that, Darlene is sure she and Eddie won't have any problems.

Outside, Darlene and Eddie walk around the house, asking all the questions serious home buyers ask about the roof and the gutters, the siding, and the air-conditioning unit. In the car, Maxine gives each of them a copy of the listing, and Darlene watches Eddie look once more at the house before he tells Maxine how much he liked it, how it really was perfect, and his tone, like before when he was talking about the woodshop, is different. It's different, Darlene thinks, because he isn't acting; he really does seem to like the house, and it surprises her. She reaches across the backseat and takes Eddie's hand in hers. He smiles at her in a way she hasn't seen in a while, and she wonders if he's feeling the same as she is.

"So," Maxine says as they pull into the parking lot of the realty office, "you guys let me know when you're planning to come back in town, and I'll make sure I have some more houses lined up for you. Maybe a few more like the last one; minus the cat, of course." Maxine laughs and looks in her rearview mirror, and Darlene can see the hope of a sale in her eyes. "Any idea when you might be ready to move?" Really, Darlene thinks, Maxine is no different than she is. She's doing what she can, seeing what she wants to see, to get what she needs.

"Soon, we hope."

Darlene tells Maxine they'll be in touch and then gives her a phone number to a voicemail she and Eddie have set up just for this. They all shake hands, and Maxine gives them her card and a folder containing the three listings and other home-buying information.

Before he even puts the key in the ignition of the car—a silver, mid-80s Cutlass Supreme, parked around the corner—Eddie asks, "How'd we do?"

Darlene thought he might say something about the moment they had in the car, but he doesn't, so she runs through the inventory in her purse: "About ten Xanax, half dozen Valium, and a bottle of Oxy." She doesn't tell him about the Ambien and the Percocet. "But, Eddie, listen—"

"A *bottle*?"

"They were in the very back of the cabinet, and the prescription is three years old. They won't miss 'em, okay? But, Eddie, I'm—"

Eddie lets out a whistle as he starts the car. "Holy shit."

"I'm done, Eddie."

"A bottle of Oxy? Fuckin-A-right we're done. That's rent for several months, plus some fun for us."

"No, I mean I'm done. With all of this." Darlene takes the bottle of Oxy out of her purse and digs around until she finds all the stray Valium and Xanax and puts them in the console cup holder.

Eddie looks at Darlene as they pull out on to the street. "Serious?"

"It's not fun anymore. I don't—"

"Is this about earlier?"

"No. Yes. It's all of it. Everything." She looks down into her purse. "You can be done with me," she says and looks into Eddie's eyes.

"You're serious."

"We can do this together," she says and wants it to be true. She starts to cry again, only this time she can't control it.

For several blocks Eddie says nothing, only looks out the windshield at the road. The pills rattle in the cup holder every time they hit a bump, and for a moment Darlene sees how easy it would be to scoop them up and throw them out the window, and she imagines each pill bouncing and tumbling down the street behind them. As they come to a stoplight at an intersection, Darlene thinks about opening the door and, without saying anything, walking away. With all the pills in the cup holder, she wonders if Eddie would try to stop her or if he'd just drive off when the light turned green. "That woodshop was great," Eddie says, interrupting Darlene's fantasy.

Eddie takes two Valium from the cup holder and holds them out to Darlene. She looks at the pills in his hand and then at Eddie.

Past him she sees a couple holding hands, walking their dog down the sidewalk. "Okay, tomorrow," he says, and suddenly the people walking are the two of them. They're smiling and laughing, Darlene sees, and she thinks *tomorrow*. When the light turns green, Eddie leaves his foot on the brake. Darlene takes the two pills out of Eddie's hand and puts them in her mouth, the bitter coating instantly absorbing into her tongue. This is the last time, she thinks, and she believes it. Her throat contracts and the pills go down. A horn honks behind them, and Eddie accelerates through the intersection.

PRESERVATION

On September 5, 1856, a mere 6 days after departing St. Louis, the Arabia *steamboat reached Westport Landing in what is now Kansas City, bound for the Nebraska Territory. The* Arabia *was loaded with nearly 150 passengers and over 200 tons of cargo, including 20,000 feet of lumber, 2,000 pairs of shoes and boots, kegs of whiskey and ale, and enough home goods (pots, pans, china, and tableware, sardines, salt pork, and other dry goods, as well as jars of pie filling and pickles, and hundreds of yards of fabrics and skins, buttons and beads, and various liniments, oils, and medicines) to resupply 16 northern frontier towns' general stores with merchandise.*

. . .

The clock in the car says we have ten minutes to get to the museum for the first tour, and we're parked in front of a converted warehouse in the River Market neighborhood several blocks away. "We've got to hustle, Jordy," I say, because he's a kid who likes to take his time. Normally, I don't mind it; he pays attention and takes things in, but at times like this it can be a pain in the ass.

When we get to the City Market, it's bustling, and I have to drag Jordy past the long line of produce-filled stalls on the west end of the wide-open U-shaped space. He keeps pulling against me, pointing and saying, "Look at all those mangoes! And at all those strawberries! And those watermelons! And tomatoes! And peppers!" Andandand. . . . I told him we could walk through and maybe grab a quick breakfast at one of the hole-in-the-wall ethnic restaurants inside the market before the museum opened—if there was time. But with leaving the house late and looking for a parking spot for almost fifteen minutes, there isn't.

I finally manage to get Jordy past the rows of tables where people are selling their produce and crafts and into the clearing on the east side in front of the Arabia Steamboat Museum. Through the glassed-in front, we can see one of the large paddle wheels from the *Arabia* turning through a pool of water. I tug one last time on Jordy's arm, and he stops.

"Dad."

"C'mon, Jordy. Or we're not going to make it."

"But, Dad, look," he says and points to a man in a wheelchair holding a sign. *Disabled Vet Please Help.*

We live in the suburbs over on the Kansas side, so I'm not sure Jordy has really seen any homeless people up close, aside from maybe someone holding a sign at a stoplight on an exit ramp. I glance at the man. His face and hair and hands are grungy, and though his clothes are filthy and threadbare, he's got his shirt buttoned all the way to the top and it looks as if it's tucked in. And he's kind of a big guy, or seems so, and his wheelchair is small and all beat to hell. He sees Jordy staring at him and wheels over to us.

"Hey, hey man, you got any spare change?"

"Sorry, we're on our way in here, and we're late," I say and check my watch. "Jordy, let's go." I walk a few steps ahead but have to come back because Jordy hasn't moved.

"What does that mean, a Vet?" Jordy asks.

"It means I served our country," the man says. "Fought in the war."

I can't really gauge the man's age, but clearly he's too young for Vietnam. I suppose it's possible he fought in Afghanistan or Iraq, though he looks old for that.

"What's wrong with your legs?" Jordy asks.

"Jesus, Jordy," I say, "don't ask that."

"I'll tell you for five bucks," the man says, and Jordy studies him for a moment, and I know what he's going to do before he even moves.

"Stop. Don't take your wallet out," I say. I know he's got a little money from his allowance because he asked me this morning if he could bring some for the Arabia gift shop, so I'm not going to stand by and let him get played.

"C'mon, it's the kid's money, let him spend it how he wants," the homeless man says to me.

"You don't have any say in this. Jordy, let's go. NOW."

"Dad," he says, "it's okay."

"I said no."

Jordy looks at me as he pulls his blue wallet from his back pocket and tears the Velcro apart and takes a five-dollar bill from inside. He's not a kid to defy authority, and the way he's looking at me, it's like he's trying to tell me that he doesn't mean to disobey me. He takes a few steps forward, extending the bill in front of him. "You don't have to tell me," he says. I have a flash of the man grabbing my son and doing . . . I don't know what, but all he does is reach out his dirty hand and take the money.

Jordy looks at the man again like he maybe sees something I don't before he turns and walks with me toward the museum doors. I put my arm around his shoulder and pull him close to me.

At the ticket counter inside the high-ceilinged lobby, I ask if we have time to make the first tour, and though we're five minutes late, the lady sells me the tickets. While I wait for the receipt to print, I watch the large paddle wheel turning in the pool, the sound of the paddles splashing into and coming out of the water filling the large space. I say to Jordy, "You didn't have to give him any money."

Jordy nods. "I know."

The woman behind the counter gives me my change, and I take a five and hold it out to Jordy. "Here, put this in your wallet."

He shakes his head. "Then it'd be like I didn't do anything."

I fold the bill and put it in my front pocket, thinking maybe I'll find some other way to give it to him, and I hand Jordy his ticket instead. We follow the arrows down the stairs to where the tour begins, and it seems we've missed the tour guide's opening remarks. Jordy leans in and gestures for me to bend down. He whispers in my ear: "Don't worry, Dad, I'll tell you what you missed."

Built in the Pennsylvania boatyard of John S. Pringle in 1853, the Arabia *steamboat was midsized at 171 feet long and 29 feet wide. A wood-burning boat, its furnaces consumed 30 cords of wood a day, fueling its 25-foot-long, iron-jacketed three-tube boilers, and its 28-foot side-wheeler paddle wheels, each with its own engine, could propel the vessel upstream at a respectable 5 miles per hour.*

The Arabia *travelled the Ohio and the Mississippi Rivers before being sold in 1856 to Captain William Terrill and William Boyd of St. Louis for $20,000. The* Arabia's *first trip on the Missouri was to Fort Pierre carrying 109 soldiers and supplies from Fort Leavenworth for Gen. Wm. S. Harney's expedition against the Sioux. In Lexington, Missouri, in early March, pro-slavery Border Ruffians seized a shipment of 100 rifles from the New England*

Emigrant Aid Company bound for abolitionist Jayhawkers in Lawrence, Kansas.

The Arabia *made 14 trips across the Missouri that year, nearly sinking in March and having to receive repairs in Portland, Missouri; a few weeks later, it blew a cylinder head and again required repairs.*

Kim and I'd planned it out: we were going to get Jordy up early on a Saturday, go to the Arabia Steamboat Museum—a place he'd gone on a field trip with his gifted class and had been begging to show us—and then hit the City Market before going for lunch, somewhere he really liked—the Rainforest Cafe at the mall, maybe, even though it was across town. After, we'd planned to tell Jordy about our decision to separate. It wasn't so much that we wanted to soften the blow for Jordy, though of course that was part of it, as it was a kind of final moment for us as a family.

But it never happened.

Early on the morning of September 5, at the Quindaro Bend near what is now Parkville, Missouri, less than five miles north of Kansas City, a walnut tree snag submerged in the turbid water tore into the Arabia's *hull, causing it to swiftly take on water. Though the river was only 15 feet deep, the river bottom was soft, and in a matter of minutes, the boat began sinking into the mud and silt.*

Kim may or may not have been cheating on me, as far as I knew, and I may or may not have been cheating on her, as far as she knew. It wasn't the physical act of cheating that did it—we were past that, I think. And that was the problem. That as far as each of us knew, we were both having affairs and that that fact alone didn't matter was everything we needed to know.

• • •

The passengers took turns with the lifeboat, and once everyone was ashore, they left on the riverbank what few belongings they had managed to salvage from the sinking Arabia *and set off for nearby Parkville. They were put up in a hotel for the night, and according to one survivor, when they returned the next morning to the site of the* Arabia's *sinking, their belongings had been pilfered by thieves in the night.*

I'd been sleeping in the spare bedroom at the end of the hall for the past few weeks. I waited to go to bed until long after Jordy was asleep, and I made sure I was up before him every morning so he wouldn't suspect anything. A couple nights before we'd planned to go to the museum, I woke in the middle of the night. I thought I'd heard a thud somewhere in the house, but it was one of those moments where I couldn't tell if the sound was real or a dream. I sat up in bed and listened, but the sound never returned.

In the morning, I found Kim sprawled in the hallway a few feet from my door. Doctors said it was an aneurysm. She'd been carrying her death around her entire life and never knew. Not that she could've done anything about it.

Here's the thing, though. The way the rooms and hallway are laid out, there's no reason she should have been on my end of that hall—Jordy's room was the other way, and there's a bathroom in the master bedroom—unless she was coming to me in the middle of the night. Did she know something was wrong? The doctors said that's not how it works, but I don't know.

The Arabia *sank so quickly in the river bottom mud that by the next morning, all that remained above water were the smokestacks and pilothouse. Soon, the Missouri devoured them, too. No one perished, yet the* Arabia's *cargo was lost, including a mule that was left tied to the deck's rail. All efforts to salvage the wreckage failed, and soon the boat was completely lost to the Missouri.*

We'd agreed not to tell anyone about the separation until after we told Jordy, so no one at the funeral—including our families—knew, though I suppose anyone close to us might've suspected we were having troubles. It felt wrong in many ways, playing the grieving husband, when what I was really feeling was anger and, oddly, betrayal. Not for any infidelities but for her forcing me to pretend, to carry all of this off by myself. A few of her coworkers looked at me in a way that made me think they knew, and maybe Kim had told them. But in their group one guy was more distraught than he should have been. I wondered if I'd ever met the man before. I didn't socialize with Kim's friends much over the years, so he didn't look familiar. He could've been her lover, I don't know. It wasn't as if I could walk up and ask him. Somehow he must've known, otherwise I doubt he would have had the balls to show up. But knowing I couldn't make a scene didn't stop me from fantasizing about kicking the shit out of him in the parking lot behind the funeral home. Despite our problems, Kim was still my wife. And she always will be, now.

Her father, Bruce, kept telling me he knew what I was going through. When he lost "his Angie" three years earlier to breast cancer, it was like "God Himself had reached in and stole my heart from my body. And now He's gone and done it again." I couldn't say much; he'd just lost his youngest daughter. But Kim's mother had battled for ten years. She was a hell of a lady, and tough, like Kim. It wasn't easy on her or anyone else, but it wasn't sudden. Everyone had a chance to say what needed to be said. There were no questions. All accounts were squared. And there wasn't an eleven-year-old left to raise.

• • •

Rapid and muddy-bottomed rivers like the Missouri often change course due to seasonal flooding, and though the story of the Arabia was told and retold until it gained near-mythical status, the exact location of the wreckage was lost. Stories persisted that over 400 barrels of whiskey sank with the Arabia, but every excavation attempt over the next hundred years failed . . .

Until, in the summer of 1988, using old river maps and newspaper clippings and a proton magnetometer, treasure hunters Bob Hawley and his sons, David and Greg, located the Arabia buried 45 feet below the ground in a farmer's cornfield over a half mile west of the Missouri River.

On November 13, 1988, the Hawley family began their excavation after promising the landowner to have it completed in time for the spring planting. The crew brought in hundreds of tons of machinery and drilled holes to find the outline of the hull. They then dug 20 wells, each over 60 feet deep, around the excavation site and installed pumps. When working at their peak, these pumps removed thousands of gallons of water per minute, siphoning it over a half mile to the Missouri River. On November 26, the crew exposed the top of the Arabia's paddle wheel 27 feet below ground level.

Over the next ten weeks, working 12-hour days, the Hawleys recovered nearly all of the cargo, as well as the one remaining engine, the boilers, and part of the rudder and stern. They completed their dig February 11, 1989, and within hours of the pumps shutting down, groundwater flooded the empty grave of the Arabia.

Jordy's been asking questions about his mother. Kim was a great mom, so I'm positive Jordy will have strong memories of her. It's just that his questions are not the kind most eleven-year-olds think to ask. Like, as a child, what did Mom want to be when she grew up? (I don't know, she never told me. But she loved her job as a middle school secretary.) What were her favorite books? (She liked *White Noise* and *The Notebook*. Go figure.) Did she and I have a song? (Yes. "Christmas Card from a Hooker in Minneapolis" by Tom Waits. It's a long story . . .) Where did we go on our honeymoon? (Branson, Missouri . . . We didn't have a lot of money.) What was her favorite band? (Honestly? Dave Matthews Band, but she always told people Wilco.) Where was her favorite place in the world? (Wherever you were, and that's the god's honest truth.) The questions come at odd moments—in the car just before dropping him off for school, playing catch in the backyard, while doing dishes after dinner—moments, it seems, when he realizes he won't ever get to ask her himself.

The Arabia Steamboat Museum opened on November 13, 1991, near the landing in Kansas City, Missouri, from which the vessel made its final departure in 1856.

The recovered cargo, concealed in the oxygen-free river mud for 132 years, was mostly preserved. Some treasures of the Arabia *include Goodyear rubber overshoes (patented 1849), Wedgwood china, firearms, jewelry, French perfume (still fragrant), wine (still potable), and perfectly preserved canned fruits and vegetables (still edible). Even the walnut snag that sank the* Arabia *was recovered.*

Once unearthed and exposed to air, the artifacts were in danger of deteriorating, so the Hawleys stored them in large water-filled tubs, cold-storage caves, and commercial restaurant freezers. They stabilized metals with tannic acid and soaked organic materials in a solution of polyethylene glycol.

A state-of-the-art preservation laboratory, housed in the museum and a part of the tour, processes over 700 objects from the Arabia *yearly. Over half the* Arabia's *cargo has been cleaned, preserved, and displayed in the museum, yet over 100 tons still remain in cold or wet storage, waiting to be treated and preserved.*

• • •

"I told you it was going to be great, didn't I?" Jordy says once we are outside the doors of the museum. He's carrying a bag from the gift shop, inside it a book about the *Arabia* steamboat and a poster-sized map of the Missouri River, Xs marking the known locations of the over four hundred steamboats that sank in the river.

"I'm glad we went," I say. "It was fun."

"I think Mom would've really liked it, too. Especially all the jewelry and Indian—I mean, Native American—beads and stuff."

He's right. Kim would've loved it. "I'm sure she would've," I say. "I'm sorry we didn't get to all come together." But as I think about it, I'm not sure. If Kim and I'd been able to go through with our plan, it would've tainted all this for Jordy forever.

We walk a little way in silence, and for no other reason than to break it, I ask, "What was your favorite part?"

"Last time it was all the preserved food, but this time I liked the snag."

"The snag?" I say.

"Yeah. I don't know. It's just, well . . ." Jordy looks down at the ground while we walk. He does this sometimes when he's thinking. "I mean, the thing that sunk the boat is in the museum. But . . . if the boat hadn't sunk, then there wouldn't be a museum . . . right? So it's, like . . . the snag is the most important thing in the whole place."

"What?" Jordy asks when I don't say anything. "Why are you smiling at me like that?"

Though our marriage was over, Kim and I were always going to be parents together, and it's moments like these that I miss her.

The market has thinned out; most of the truck farms and the Mennonites selling their breads and pies have packed up as have the craftspeople hawking their goods. The larger, permanent produce stalls around the edges are still open, and though many of them are beginning to close, I ask if Jordy wants to walk through. He does, so we head to the north side toward the river.

At one stall we watch a moment as two Latin men with machetes cut the tops off fresh coconuts for people to drink the water. The coconuts are green and somewhat oblong and look nothing like the brown hairy kind in grocery stores. I let Jordy pick one out for us to share. We watch as one of the men expertly lops off just enough of the green outer shell to poke a long straw through. I pay and let Jordy take the first drink. He does and smiles. "Good," he says. I take a drink, and it's sweet and smooth.

We walk through the rest of the market, passing the coconut back and forth between us. Near the exit, Jordy stops in front of a long table of spices manned by an older Arab gentleman. The air around the table is a heady mix, simultaneously appealing and slightly nauseating. Jordy looks at what must be well over fifty spice bins, seeming to study the exotic names, *Star Anise, Cardamom, Fenugreek, Orris Root, Zedoary,* and I see that the man has stopped packing up so Jordy can continue to look. I start to say something, but the man smiles and waves his hand at me as if to say, "Let the boy look." I nod my thanks, and after a moment Jordy is ready to keep walking.

Outside the market, we start up the hill toward where we parked. Few cars remain in the lots, and there are spots open on the street. Just before we get to our car, Jordy says, "Dad? I've been wanting to ask you something."

"What is it?" I say and take my keys out of my pocket and press the unlock button on the key fob.

Jordy goes to the passenger side and steps up on the curb, and over the top of the car, I watch his shoulders rise as he takes a deep breath. "Why were you sleeping in the spare bedroom?"

"What do you mean?" I say, but I know exactly what he means, I just had no idea he knew. I open my car door and get in.

"On the night Mom died," he says as he settles into his seat and waits for me to say something. I can't face him, so I stare through the windshield at the skyscrapers visible through the gap between the buildings. "The spare bedroom door was open, and the bed was messy. And your watch was on the nightstand."

In the chaos of that morning, I didn't even think to close the door. He must've looked in the room sometime that day while I was dealing with the hospital and the funeral home. I don't know what to say; I don't want to lie to Jordy, but I can't tell him the truth, either.

"Dad?" he says again.

"Jordy, I . . ."

"No, Dad, look," he says, and I turn my head and follow where he's pointing out his window. There, at the mouth of the alley, is the wheelchair-bound homeless man from in front of the Arabia museum, only he's walking on two completely functional legs.

"Sonofabitch," I say. Jordy and I watch him cross the sidewalk and stroll directly in front of our car. I honk and he stops, squinting and leaning his head down slightly to see us behind the windshield. Then it seems he recognizes us because he straightens up quickly. He stands a moment and we stare at each other. Then he smiles and shrugs his shoulders before walking away.

"His shoes," Jordy says.

"What?" I say and look at the man walking away. He's got on broken-down white sneakers. A paralyzed person's shoes aren't going to be worn out. "Shit. You knew?"

"Not really, but I noticed them."

"Then why'd you give him money?"

"Maybe he needed it," he says.

We sit together in the car, Jordy's unanswered question still hanging in the air, and watch the man walk up the street where he disappears into another alley.

ABSOLUTION

The video, shot from only a few rows up, comes in just at the end of my instructions, which sound garbled through the cheap PA. The camera work is shaky, jerking from the backs of people's heads to the water-stained drop ceiling and then to the large bingo board on the wall, before finally settling on the ring in the center of the room. For the next four minutes, everything is as steady and in focus as the primitive cell phone camera will allow.

You might think you're watching some kind of underground "fight club," but it's a professional boxing match, fully sanctioned by the state of Kansas. And you probably don't notice me, but I'm there, right in the middle of the ring. It was my 137th bout, and after that many, you get a feeling about certain fighters. There's something that you can't see from anywhere but inside the ring. It's in the eyes, and I know it when I see it, and I saw it that night in the eyes of Manuel Cardenza. It's an unsettling coldness that you can't shake, not unlike, I imagine, looking into the eyes of a predator in the wild.

At the left of the screen, Cardenza's opponent, Jimmy O'Rourke, bounces in his corner, rolls his neck, and repeatedly taps his gloves to his face. To the untrained observer, he probably looks more the fighter than Cardenza, who stands coolly in his corner, slightly shifting his weight back and forth, occasionally shaking out his arms. Though both men are welterweights, O'Rourke looks considerably bigger, both taller and more muscularly defined than Cardenza, whose body looks more like that of a fifteen-year-old boy than a professional boxer. O'Rourke's trying hard to look the part, and he might've even fooled you. But not me. His movements, unlike Cardenza's, are mannered. What you're watching is a man struggling to hide his fear.

At the bell, O'Rourke barges out of his corner and immediately starts throwing looping combinations. Cardenza slips a few of the punches, but several land. Of the five fights O'Rourke has won, it's clear this was how. But Cardenza, though his professional record is only marginally better at 8–0, fought 114 amateur fights in Mexico, and you can see by the way he relaxes as he covers that he's in no real danger of being hurt by O'Rourke's wild flailing punches. Every chance Cardenza gets, he clinches, leaning on O'Rourke's arms, forcing me to separate them.

After a little over a minute of this, the crowd begins to boo, heckling Cardenza for holding and not fighting back. *We didn't pay to watch you two dance!* someone in the crowd shouts. O'Rourke is already deadweight when I next break them apart. He's an impressive physical specimen, but he's a long way from fighting shape. His mouth is open, and he's sucking air like a fish on a dock, and it's every bit as useless. When I clap my hands to signal for them to continue, Cardenza pounces, throwing two quick jabs and a straight right, landing all three flush. O'Rourke stumbles back, stunned, and leans against the ropes. He manages to get his hands up, but Cardenza slips two more jabs and another straight right between his gloves. Then the real assault begins. Every one of Cardenza's punches lands exactly where he intends: three left hooks to the body, a right uppercut, and a quick left hook to the head followed by a straight right through O'Rourke's failing guard. Cardenza pummels him against the ropes, and he's so efficient: he never loses control, never lets his punches swing wide. He's not trying to score a knockout; he's dismantling his opponent with perfect, machinelike precision. And that's what I can't take my eyes off of. Not now, not then.

It's something, watching myself in the ring watching Cardenza continue to land blow after punishing blow, his punches the only thing keeping O'Rourke upright. *Oh my God, stop the fight!* a person near the camera yells. In the moment, I knew I should stop the fight—it's my job to protect both fighters—but the devastating grace with which Cardenza was ruining O'Rourke rooted me to my spot.

The crowd's cheering builds then turns to an eerie murmuring, and then it's no longer a single voice shouting for the fight to stop. But there on the screen and here in my chair, I don't move, except to get a better angle in the ring. A towel sails over the ropes from O'Rourke's corner and lands at my feet, and when I still don't move, his manager jumps up on the edge of the ring. You can hear him shouting at me on the video as he shakes the top rope. Cardenza continues to hammer his opponent. Finally, mercifully for me then, and now, Cardenza's manager scrambles through the ropes and puts his arms around his fighter, pulling him from O'Rourke. As soon as the punches stop, O'Rourke crumples to the canvas like a wet rag. Only then do I see myself waving my arms over my head, signaling the end of the fight.

O'Rourke's cornermen rush into the ring, and in a matter of seconds he's on a stretcher and paramedics are wheeling him out of the building. You can't see it on the video, but even after that beating there was only a trickle of blood from his nose. Probably broken, I remember thinking. But it was the swelling of the brain that did it. Like how the screen goes black when the camera is switched off.

IF THERE COULD'VE BEEN ANOTHER WAY, I WISH THAT'S HOW IT'D BEEN

Charlie had his thumb on the down arrow of the elevator, pushing so hard the skin around his nail turned white. The ink probably hadn't dried on his divorce papers in the law office from which he'd just fled. He couldn't believe Rebecca had brought *him*— Franklin. Charlie had met him once or twice at department gatherings; he was on Rebecca's dissertation committee, and she'd made a point to introduce the two of them. Charlie didn't care for him then, but he didn't much care for any of the faculty or Rebecca's grad student friends. As an elementary school PE teacher, he just didn't have much in common with any of them. He drank light beer, watched ESPN, liked good old American food, and aside from *Sports Illustrated*, he didn't read. He got paid to wear track pants and play games with kids all day. He loved it, and he believed what he did mattered, but around people like Franklin he couldn't help but see himself as second-rate, unworthy of the esteem given to other educators. He knew despite what these people said, they didn't respect him, but it had never mattered because he knew Rebecca did. Until today when he saw Franklin with her at the table.

He knew that this meeting, outside of any chance encounters, would probably be the last time he would see Rebecca—that's why he'd insisted on it, in fact—but as much as he wanted to look at her, for her to see in his eyes how hurt he was, he couldn't manage it. Charlie'd been on time, but when he got to the law office, everyone was already seated around the table waiting for him. He felt like a fool in his nylon pants and elementary school–logoed polo, his ID badge clipped to his shirt, his whistle still around his neck, as he sat across from the professionally dressed couple—Franklin in a navy blue blazer and white button-down, the top opened just enough to let a few silver chest hairs sprout out the neck; Rebecca in a loose-fitting off-white blouse. In his anger and embarrassment, he signed where his lawyer told him to without looking up from the papers. When it was over, Charlie stood and walked out the door without even speaking to his lawyer.

He held his finger on the button though he knew it wouldn't make the elevator arrive any faster. He saw an exit sign at the other end of the hall, and after waiting what felt like several minutes, he let go of the button and started quickly across the hall, his pants swishing in the quiet space. But as he approached the law office door, he heard voices—Franklin's and Rebecca's—and he didn't want to be caught running for the stairs, so he turned back to the elevator and prayed the doors would open before they could catch him.

Charlie heard the elevator rising to his floor at the same time the door to the law office opened down the hall. "C'mon, goddammit," he said. When the elevator dinged and the doors finally opened, Charlie rushed in and was hammering the close button with his finger before the doors were even completely open.

"Hold the door, please!"

It was Franklin's voice. Charlie continued to jab the button, but it didn't cooperate. He heard Franklin's feet thumping on the carpet as the door started to close. Just when Charlie thought he'd made it, Franklin stuck his hand between the doors and they bounced back open. He looked surprised when he saw it was Charlie in the elevator.

"Let's just wait for the next one, Franklin," Rebecca said from behind.

"I'm sure Charlie doesn't mind," he said. "Right, Charlie?"

You could damn well bet that Charlie minded, but before he could say anything, Franklin, holding the door open, said, "Here you go, Becky."

Becky? Rebecca had always hated being called Becca or Becky and insisted people call her by her full name. Charlie moved to the back corner of the elevator and leaned against the wall. And it was a good thing, too, because when he saw Rebecca step into the elevator, hand wrapped under her gently swollen abdomen, his legs went wobbly. With the way they'd been seated at the table in the lawyer's office, Charlie hadn't noticed Rebecca's condition, but then he hadn't even thought to look.

Charlie opened his mouth to speak, but the only sound he could make was a kind of exhalation, as if he'd had the wind knocked out of him. Charlie tried to take a deep breath, but it caught in his throat. As much as he'd come to hate Rebecca in the last few months, he couldn't just turn off his feelings for her. They'd been together since Charlie's junior year in college. Rebecca was a freshman when they met, and he liked to tell people that he'd known she was "the one" when he first saw her, but in reality all he knew when he first saw her was that he wanted to get her naked. The feelings came later, but they came quickly. And the thought of her having someone else's—Franklin's—baby . . . he became nauseous and put his hands on his knees and lowered his head. He took a couple slow deep breaths as he focused on his chrome whistle pendulously hanging from his neck.

"Charlie? Are you all right?" Rebecca said and stepped to the middle of the elevator.

"You're having his fucking baby?" Charlie said, looking up, a kind of unexpected keening in his voice, and gestured at Franklin. "*Him*? I thought this was just a goddamn affair, not—"

"I'll not stand here and have you disrespecting the mother of my child," Franklin said and pointed his finger at Charlie as the elevator doors closed and it began its descent. "Do you hear me, Charlie? I'll . . . I'll throw down if I need to!" Franklin said the words as if he were trying them on, seeing how they fit.

Charlie knew that despite Franklin being the bigger man, it was all posturing and so ignored him. A few years ago—hell, a few minutes ago—Charlie would've stomped Franklin into the floor, given him what he was begging for, what Charlie knew Franklin in some way expected from a guy like him. But the impulse that used to come on so rapidly just wasn't there. It was as if he understood, all at once while staring at the elevator floor, that the thing he used to be willing to fight for had vanished, and the sensation for Charlie was physical, like a kind of shrinking in his gut.

In the churning mess of Charlie's thoughts, one detached itself from the fray and settled squarely in his mind: When was the last time they'd had sex?

Charlie raised up and looked at Rebecca. When she'd come to get the last of her stuff from their house—a box of books, some heirloom dishes her mother had given her, and the rest of her clothes—they'd recklessly fucked on their bedroom floor, Rebecca sobbing as she walked out of their house for the last time. When was that, exactly? Charlie frantically tried to do the math in his head. Three months ago? Four?

Rebecca stared at Charlie, and for just an instant in her wide and wet eyes, he recognized a look he'd seen only once, years before, when Rebecca had received a call that her father had had a heart attack. He remembered the look: it was fear and shock and sadness and a dozen other emotions, but as quick as it appeared there in the elevator, it was gone. Then, as if she'd read the question that had surfaced in Charlie's mind, she very slightly shook her head and cautiously placed her hand atop her belly. He stared at her, trying to somehow call back that look and the emotions it held, but all that was left were Rebecca's blue eyes staring out from above the dusting of freckles on her cheeks.

"Are you sure?" he said.

"Now just what kind of question is that?" Franklin said.

"I was talking to *Rebecca*," Charlie said, "not you."

"Charlie . . ."

"Is it mine?"

"Just wait a goddamn minute!" Franklin said.

Rebecca slowly shook her head. "No," she said. "It isn't."

"But what about—"

The elevator dinged at the fourth floor. When the doors opened, a janitor with a shaved head and tattoo of a spider on his neck wheeled a mop bucket into the elevator without even looking. He had headphones in his ears, and he startled when he looked up. "Shit," he said. He reached down and touched a button on his music player. "Sorry. Didn't expect anyone to be here." He pressed the "3" button and turned to face the front.

There was a moment of awkward silence while the four of them waited for the doors to close and the elevator to continue its descent. When it did, Charlie stared at Rebecca, waiting for her to say something.

"He doesn't know?" Charlie said.

"What don't I know? What are you talking about?"

"Nothing, Franklin," Rebecca said.

"I want to know right now what's going on."

"Franklin, *please*," Rebecca said. "Stop."

The janitor cleared his throat as the elevator jolted softly to a stop and the doors dinged open. In a hurry to get out, he pushed his mop bucket quickly over the gap, but the wheels caught and gray water slopped onto the floor. "*Motherfucker*," he said under his breath.

Charlie, Rebecca, and Franklin watched the janitor sopping up the water with his dirty mop until the doors closed and the elevator dipped.

Charlie looked again at Rebecca, waiting for her to speak. "I see," he said after a moment. "Well—"

"We're getting married," Rebecca said, interrupting Charlie. Her voice was steady, calm.

"What?"

"Soon, before the baby comes," she said, and Franklin put his hand on her shoulder. "I wanted you to hear that from me. I'm sorry you had to find out about everything like this. This isn't how I would've wanted it." She reached across her body and put her hand atop Franklin's.

"Then how? If not this way," Charlie said.

"You know what I meant, Charlie," Rebecca said as the elevator settled to a stop and the doors opened to the lobby.

She stepped out, Franklin trailing behind her. She took a few steps and stopped, turning back to Charlie, still inside the elevator. "If there could've been another way, I wish that's how it'd been."

Charlie listened to the sound of Rebecca's shoes snick-tocking on the lobby floor. When the doors began to close, Charlie stabbed his hand between them, and as they jerked open, he lunged out. Rebecca and Franklin were across the lobby, just approaching the revolving doors at the front of the building. When Franklin placed his hand on the small of Rebecca's back and led her to the door, Charlie lifted the whistle from where it hung at his chest and brought it to his lips. He blew a long, shrill note that echoed off the floor and walls of the high-ceilinged lobby. Both Rebecca and Franklin ducked their heads in alarm and turned to Charlie. He stood, whistle still in his mouth, looking at Rebecca, but she was too far away for him to see into her eyes. She dropped her head and stepped through the revolving door. Charlie blew another note, softer, holding it until it rattled to a tinny, feeble end.

PINCHBECK

Wild Bill is getting married tomorrow, so in this afternoon's show everyone hits their marks, trying to prove they can fill Wild Bill's boots. Fourth of July is easily the biggest weekend of the season for Old Town Abilene's "Gunfight on Main Street." We'd heard that Bill—the guy's name who plays Wild Bill is actually Bill, I'm not making this up—was going to handpick one of us to fill in. Wild Bill is the only set part in the show; the rest of us rotate between the other roles. Bill's a history professor at Wesleyan over in Salina, and he's been playing Wild Bill for years. It's not some summertime hobby for him; he takes it seriously, and all of us know this.

As Cowboy 3, I look like an extra right out of an episode of *Gunsmoke*, with dusty dungarees and boots, a denim Western-style shirt and red bandana. I'm leaning against the split-pine porch rail of the dry goods store, which doubles as the Old Town gift shop before and after the show. Across the wide dirt lane, Cowboy 5 hitches an old deaf horse to the rail in front of the false Post Office, Villains 1 and 2 hang around the horse stable, and several pairs of women in long, rough-cut dresses and off-white bonnets crisscross the lane. The set is modeled after the real 1870s Main Street in Abilene (two of the structures are even authentic): low-slung buildings with second-story false fronts, wooden porches, hitching posts, and even water troughs, like the stylized versions we recognize from TV shows and movies.

Unlike in the theater, where the stage lights keep us from seeing the audience, here, under the never-ending Kansas sky, they are right in front of us, corralled by a split-rail fence in front of the Bull's Head Saloon in the middle of Main Street. When I'm playing one of the lesser roles, like Cowboy 3, I like to watch them watch the show. The most faithful are probably old folks, those bused in on day trips from retirement homes in Topeka, Manhattan, and Salina, and those of the over-the-road America bus tours that stop to see the Eisenhower Library, which is conveniently just across the street. I'd venture to guess that most of the rest are either on their way to Kansas City or Denver, and we're just a kind of pit stop, a place to get lunch and stretch their legs, and *Well look at that, an Old West show, and it starts in twenty minutes . . .*

The attendance is sparse, especially for a Friday afternoon. One false front down from where I stand, Wild Bill and Phil Coe will have their first encounter of the show. When so few are watching, the show can feel puny, and unfortunately, we sometimes surrender to it. But not with the role of Wild Bill on the line. Cowboy 3 isn't an integral part, so as bad as I want to show off and prove I can play Wild Bill, there won't be an opportunity to stand out. All

I have to do is run down to the Bull's Head and stand around the fringes of Wild Bill's group when he throws out Coe.

It's a shame, too, with Clare coming out for the weekend. She's the event coordinator at the Plaza Branch of the Kansas City Public Library, and they launched a new Writer's Reading Series this summer. Since she'll be on maternity leave after the first of the year, she's trying to get as far ahead at work as she can. This will be the only time she'll have to see me, and I want nothing more than to be the star and, as a final thank-you for all her faith in me and my career, to show her one more time that I do have some talent, that I really can act, even if it is in a silly Old West show. See, I decided a week or so ago to quit the show, but I haven't told anyone yet.

Back in the spring, I auditioned for several roles, but this was the only one I got. Clare pushed me to take the job, said I couldn't pass up an acting gig, regardless of what it was, because who knows what it might lead to? Though I knew it was unlikely this would lead to something (okay, impossible), I took the job in Abilene for the summer. Then we found out she was pregnant. It took us both off guard; it wasn't that we were opposed to having a baby, it's just that it was always in the future, after my career had taken off and we were married. Deep down I think we both knew, but didn't want to admit, that waiting for my career to "take off" meant we probably weren't going to have children. Honestly, at first I harbored quite a bit of resentment, not for Clare or even for the baby. Just a vague, selfish bitterness. Pushing me to take this job was, I think, Clare's way of ignoring the situation and my resentment, at least for a while. She'd invested so much of herself in my career that I'm not sure she was ready to come to terms with what her pregnancy meant, either. Clare insisted she'd be fine without me for a couple months, that it was still early enough in the pregnancy. I wasn't so sure, but that didn't stop me from coming out here.

But all that was before the show even started for the summer. After the first performance, I knew I was finished. It wasn't so much that I thought the show was beneath me, it was that I realized I was at the stage in my career where this kind of show was a good fit for me. It took me a few weeks to finally admit it to myself, but I knew. The show wasn't bad as small town reenactments go, but I recognized, probably far later than I should have, that this gig wasn't about taking the next step in my career, it was about taking the last. Clare never would have asked me to quit; it had to be my decision alone. And it was for the very best reason: I was going to be a father. Once I'd accepted that, the resentment fell away, and while I was still scared, I was excited, too. And, after I'd made my decision, the show took on a wistful, nostalgic quality that I came to enjoy. To top it all off, starting in the fall, I've got a job teaching dramatic arts at a magnet school in Kansas City. My old college roommate teaches math there and he got me in touch with the principal. For the first time in my life I'll be gainfully, and steadily, employed with benefits and everything. I'm going to surprise Clare with the news when she gets here.

On cue, there's a commotion and Coe comes tumbling through the swinging saloon doors and sprawls, face down in the dirt. That stunt is a big hit when there is more of an audience, but as I jog into the scene I hear only a single "Oh" escape someone's mouth.

According to the script, Wild Bill waits a few beats before stepping through the saloon doors and looking at Coe who, with the help of Villains 1 and 2, is dusting himself off. Bill's an imposing figure in his buckskin coat, with the pearl-handled Navy Colts tucked cavalry-style in the wide leather belt, and the long mustache and hair and the round, flat-topped sombrero. Even though I've seen it in every show, it's impressive how he commands everyone's attention. Bill's a barrel-chested man, considerably heavier than Wild Bill was, but it doesn't take away from the feeling of the show. In fact, it probably helps him live up to the legend.

In a booming voice, Wild Bill says, "Phil Coe, I should order you arrested for disturbing the peace of the good people of Abilene."

Coe was a notorious gunfighter out of Texas, and each of us plays him a little differently, but Kevin, the guy playing Coe today, lays it on thick—too thick for my taste. Hunching his shoulders a little too villainously and scrunching his face at Wild Bill, Coe points and says, "Marshal 'Wild Bill' Hickok, you ain't nothin' but a scoundrel and a cheat. I saw you deal from the bottom."

Bill replies in a practiced, measured way. "I did no such thing. There are witnesses."

Kevin, still overplaying Coe, says, "I'll get you, 'Wild Bill.' I'm the best gunman this side of the Rio Grande. Once I killed a crow on the wing."

For the final (probably apocryphal) line of the exchange, the one people remember when they leave, Bill turns up the cowboy cool and, in a cross between a stylized John Wayne and a gritty Clint Eastwood, says, "Did the crow have a pistol? Was he shooting back? 'Cause I will be."

With that, Phil Coe and Villains 1 and 2 slink away muttering to each other, and Wild Bill says to everyone, "A round on the marshal!" All those who have come out of the Bull's Head let out some kind of whoop or cheer and go back in the bar clapping each other on the back and praising the good marshal. Wild Bill steps off the porch and approaches the audience, breaking the proverbial fourth wall. Normally, there is a kind of rock star scene where everyone pushes forward and surrounds him, but with so few people it looks odd and a little pathetic. But despite the awkwardness of the situation, Wild Bill doesn't disappoint. He regales everyone with the same gambling and gunfighting and Civil War scouting tales he tells every show, yet it doesn't feel at all tired. It's as if Bill's incapable of phoning it in.

After five minutes of chatting and even having his picture "made" next to a few people ("What is that contraption you have there? A camera you say? I'll have to send to Kansas City for one of them shiny newfangled things"), it's time for Coe and Villains 1 and 2 to return and ambush the marshal.

In three separate alleys between the buildings, Coe and Villains 1 and 2 creep toward Main Street. Wild Bill says to everyone, "I best go make good on my promise," and turns back toward the bar, which is the cue for Coe and the Villains to come storming out of their respective alleys, guns blazing from three directions. Someone in the audience lets out a cry of surprise at the popping of the gunfire, the ends of the gun barrels flashing with movie loads. From where I take cover at the side of the saloon, I see Wild Bill turn, draw both his guns in one motion, and fire first upon Villain 1 who falls in a heap at the mouth of one alley, and then at Villain 2 who meets his death in the middle of the lane as he charges. Though I've been in the show for weeks, I haven't gotten used to the ringing in my ears from the gunfire. Because of all the commotion, no one stops to wonder how Wild Bill managed to dodge all the bullets aimed his way. Wild Bill stands, both guns at the ready, as Coe steps out from behind a post and walks slowly toward him. Both Wild Bill and Coe have their guns trained on the other in the way of the mythical Wild West showdown. Coe stops thirty or forty paces short. "This is over, Coe. You're under arrest," Wild Bill announces. Kevin plays the next part well, I have to admit, as he, Coe, stands for several seconds to build the tension of the moment before making as if to place his gun on the ground. Since everyone is so caught up in the drama, no one notices Coe's wildly telegraphed move as he comes out of his crouch and raises his gun to fire. But before he can even get his gun to chest level he's cut down by the quick-drawing Wild Bill. The reenactment ends there, and Wild Bill, the good marshal of Abilene, is the hero and protector of the town.

The show might seem artless to some, but it's really not that bad. And, a gunfight between Wild Bill and Phil Coe did happen in Abilene in 1871. Like any actor worth his salt, I did my research. There are several versions of how the shooting occurred; most agree that Coe shot at a stray dog, and when Hickok demanded he surrender his firearms (they were prohibited in the city limits),

Coe turned his gun on Hickok, "forcing" Hickok to shoot him. But there's more to it than that. These men didn't like each other; they'd had several run-ins during Hickok's short tenure as marshal, and it was rumored that when they found out they were "courting" the same woman each man vowed to kill the other. Some say Coe gathered a rowdy group of cowboys and was planning to ambush Hickok, but Hickok caught wind of it and cornered Coe and shot him. Whatever the details, there's a key part the Old Town Abilene's "Gunfight on Main Street" leaves out: after shooting Coe, Hickok accidentally shot and killed a deputy marshal who was coming to his aid.

Conveniently, Coe and the fallen Villains are far enough away to spare the audience the brutality of deaths by gunshot and the production from having to deal with squibs and fake blood. As the smoke from the ends of Wild Bill's pearl-handled Colts clears, everyone stands silently, perhaps surprised at how fast everything has occurred. Despite its budget, the show creates a strong illusion, and it usually takes a moment before someone in the audience claps, bringing everyone back to the real world. Wild Bill holsters his Colts and walks to the split-rail fence. He raises a boot to the lower rail and, as usual, soaks up the praise of the small but now enthusiastic crowd.

After the show, I sit in front of my locker in the makeshift dressing room in back of the saloon wondering how I'm going to tell everyone about my decision to quit when Bill pops his head in and asks to see me. Bill has never called me out front before, but I've heard stories. Sometimes it's a pat on the back; other times it's a reprimand for missing a mark. As I leave the room, a few of the guys nod and smile but some avert their eyes. Bill's in the saloon still dressed as Wild Bill, sitting at the long mahogany bar that's been aged and lacquered to look authentic. In front of him sit two shot glasses and a three-quarters-full bottle of Early Times. He motions for me to sit on the stool next to him.

"Early Times?" I say as I pull out the stool and sit.

"I know. But it seemed appropriate," Bill says and twists off the cap. "I saw the way you were watching today. I know you haven't gotten to show it yet, but you're a good actor, Ty."

"Thanks, Bill." I'm momentarily caught off guard. "It means a lot." And it does. Bill isn't really an actor, at least not in the way I've always considered myself, but he has a quality people respond to, and I respect him.

Bill pours out two shots and raises his glass. "Wild Bill's yours for the weekend. You earned it," he says and waits for me to take up my glass. I can't tell him that I'm quitting, not now, because though I've come to terms with my decision, I want this role. What better way to go out than as Wild Bill Hickok? And with Clare coming for the weekend, I couldn't have planned it better.

I clink my glass against his. I decide then that I'll just tell everyone after the show Sunday afternoon. "It'd be an honor," I say and down the shot. Bill laughs as I hack and cough my way through the burning in my throat and nose. "Jesus," I say, "that shit's awful."

"You're Wild Bill, now, so you're gonna have to drink like him." Bill pours another shot for each of us.

Bill keeps pouring shots, and before I know it, we're both shouting toasts.

"I'm Wild-fucking-Bill!"

"I'm getting married this weekend!"

"I'm going to be a father!"

I haven't said it out loud before, and even though it still scares me, I've never felt better about anything. My announcement brings a giant clap on the back from Bill followed by more shots.

Later that night in my suite at the Extended Stay just north of I-70, I get the idea that I need to see what I look like as Wild Bill. My face isn't as hawkish, but I'm tall and thin enough to pull it off. With the hat, wig, and mustache, the buckskin coat and the Colts, I look more like Wild Bill than Bill does. I go through Wild Bill's lines half a dozen times in front of the bathroom mirror, drunkenly experimenting with my delivery, while I wait for Clare to call to tell me what time she's planning to get here in the morning. Before I make my way to bed, I look at the most recent picture she sent me of her belly. It's taped to the bathroom mirror next to the first sonogram picture she sent a few weeks ago. I know I should have been there for Clare and for the doctor appointments; I offered to take a day or two off to come back to Kansas City, but she insisted everything was fine. In the picture of her belly, Clare has her shirt pulled up to just below her breasts, and because she's petite, I can already see where her stomach is swelling. The sonogram picture is gray and grainy, and as hard as I've tried, I can't see anything but a small splotch of lighter gray in the middle. But it's okay; I know the baby is in there somewhere.

When it gets past the time I think Clare will call, I take my cell phone off the nightstand and call her. It rings several times before going to voicemail. Her voice tells me she isn't available to take my call, and can I please leave a message? So, after the tone I say, "What's shakin', baby?" Wild Bill's mustache scratches against the phone, so I pull it from my face. "Owww. Goddamn mustache." My tongue feels thick and a little unruly in my mouth. "Clare, baby, I'm Wild Bill," I say, "and I'm drunk. And I'm going to be a father. I'm Wild Bill and I'm drunk and I'm going to be a father," I say one more time. When I can't think of anything else, I say, "I love you."

Crossing the I-70 overpass this morning into town, head a little foggy from the whiskey, I look first to the wide expansive prairie to the west, unfurled all the way to the horizon, and then east across the rolling Flint Hills, the grass tinted gold beneath the morning sun. I've been here for almost eight weeks, but I still can't manage to get over the bare, stripped feeling that being out here gives a person. I'm completely exposed and unsheltered like few other places I can imagine. I think about Clare driving through the vast openness, the baby safely tucked in her belly,

Clare safely tucked and belted in the car, and though I know they're safe, I worry about her and the baby in a way I've never worried about anything before. This exposed feeling, this unsettling fear is, I understand for the first time, what being a father is going to be like.

As the final preparations for the show are underway, I begin to wonder if Clare is going to make it before we start. I was in the shower when she called this morning, and she left me a message saying she'd be here by showtime. Her message was short and her voice a little clipped, like she was in a hurry.

As I'm fitting the mustache on my face, one of the other actors pops his head in the dressing room and says it's time to go. I put on Wild Bill's hat, tuck the Colts into my belt, and head into the saloon.

As soon as Kevin sees me, he nods and everyone in the room starts making noise, shouting and stomping their boots on the floor. Backing up to get a running start, Kevin hurls himself through the swinging saloon doors, over the porch, and out onto the dirt lane in front of the crowd. I hear a few shout in surprise and some even laugh. In the second that follows Kevin tumbling through the doors, I think I see Clare in the audience. I hurry outside and stumble, catching myself against the knotted post. I scan the crowd but can't find her. Kevin and the two Villains are staring at me, and then I realize that everyone in the crowd is staring at me, too. Not even a minute into the scene, and I've already blown the timing. I tug on the bottom of my buckskin coat and say, "Phil Coe, I should arrest you for ordering—order you arrested for disturbing the people—the peace of the people of Abilene."

"Marshal 'Wild Bill' Hickok, you ain't nothin' but a scoundrel and a cheat. I saw you deal from the bottom," Kevin says, playing Coe even more villainously, clearly pissed he wasn't picked to play Wild Bill.

"I did not," I say slowly to get back into the rhythm of the dialog. "There are witnesses." I gesture to the crowd, who applaud softly.

"I'll get you, 'Wild Bill.' I'm the best gunman this side of the Rio Grande. Once I killed a crow on the wing."

"Did that crow have a pistol?" I say, savoring the line, making it my own. "Was he shooting back? 'Cause you can bet I'll be."

After Kevin and the two Villains have walked away and I've called for a round of drinks, I take a deep breath, happy that I recovered from my opening blunder. Then, out of the corner of my eye, I see Clare walking from the parking lot around toward the edge of the split-rail corral where the crowd waits for Wild Bill, me, to talk to them. She looks different somehow, and I know that part of it is not having seen her in person for the last two months; but that's not it. She's overdressed for the heat, long yoga pants and a baggy zip-up hoodie, but it's something else entirely. She's walking with her shoulders hunched forward, like she's trying not to be noticed. Though she's still at some distance, I expect to be able to see her bump a little better, even with the sweatshirt, but as she comes closer I still can't see it. She stops just outside the crowd, and I make eye contact with her. She looks surprised, as if she didn't intend for me to see her yet, and her eyes and nose are puffy and red.

I circle to the side of the corral and she meets me at the edge. I smile at her, but the look on her face doesn't change. "Ty," she says, and tears pool in her eyelids before rolling down her cheeks.

I can't move and I can barely breathe when I realize what's wrong. I search her face for answers to all the questions running through my mind—*when? what happened? how? are you all right? when were you going to tell me?*—but her face doesn't give up any. I move toward her again, but I see her eyes sweep around to the crowd watching us. I forgot they were even here, that I was even doing this show. Clare looks at me again and shakes her head. "Ty," she says again. Before I can say anything, someone steps out of the saloon and shouts, "What about that round, Marshal? Ain't you going to come make good?"

I turn from Clare, to the saloon, to everyone in the crowd. It's clear from the looks on their faces they don't know what's going on. And I don't either, not anymore.

From across the lane, Villains 1 and 2 come bursting from their respective alleys, guns popping. Some people scream and duck at the sound of the gunfire, and though I'm supposed to draw on the men and cut them down, I only stand and watch. Even from this distance, I can see both Villains are confused. They know they are supposed to fall from my gunshots, but I haven't drawn my weapons, let alone fired upon them. When their guns are empty, they stop running toward me and stand, arms at their sides, in the middle of the lane. I see Kevin poke his head from the alley before stepping out. He looks as confused as everyone else. He has to know the show has completely gone off the rails, but he draws his guns and seems to be going through with the act. He walks to within ten yards and stops, guns at his side.

I look down at my costume, the fake buckskin coat and the replica Colts and then at the false fronts of the Main Street set. I shift my weight and feel the pull of the Colts at my waist. When I draw them from my belt, someone in the crowd gasps. I raise the guns at Kevin, who, caught up in his character, flinches and aims his guns at me. For a moment we remain there, barely thirty feet apart, guns trained on one another. Before I cock the hammers and raise both guns to my temples, I think of emptying all twelve impotent cylinders at Kevin and at the crowd, which seems to have swelled around me. I look across to Clare, and she's raised one of her hands to her face. Her eyes are wide, and she's crying. Everyone is silent as I stand there in the middle of the lane with the guns to my head, and I think again about the grainy black-and-white sonogram picture. I squeeze the triggers and the simultaneous gunshots blast this from my mind, and I'm left with a searing pain in my temples and a torrid ringing in my ears as I fall backward. I hit the ground hard but don't even hear a thud. In the air above me, the smell of cordite mixes with that of singed wig-hair. My right ear feels liquidy, and I can't hear anything but the deafening tone. From my back, I watch a puffy white cloud slowly dissolve as it moves across the wide open Kansas sky.

LUCK

At the end of the shift, Briggs, the supervisor, came in with a copy of Hamlin Rankin's order and a government-issued check for fifteen dollars and slid them both across the table.

"New Guy, here's Shitbird's order."

Collins had been there for six months, but he was still New Guy to Briggs and everyone else. In just that short time, he'd already seen half a dozen men start, but no one stayed on the job long. Those men weren't called anything; they were lucky to even be acknowledged. He knew that New Guy was a step toward the guys learning his name, trusting him, which, he'd learned quickly, was paramount for corrections officers. But that wasn't something he was necessarily happy about.

"I already clocked out," Collins said and started across the room that doubled as a kind of debriefing space and dressing room with lockers on three sides.

"I'll approve the OT."

Collins grabbed the paper and read the flowing handwriting on the five lines of the order:

> *Sea Bass (pan-seared) with Garlic Cream Sauce*
> *Filet Mignon*
> *1 Can of Royal Crown Cola*
> *1 bag of Guy's Barbeque Potato Chips*
> *1 King Size Reese's Peanut Butter Cup*

Collins wondered if Rankin had ever eaten sea bass, because he hadn't. "What do you want me to do with this?"

"Tomorrow's the big day," Briggs said and pointed to the dry-erase calendar where the month's happenings were set: inmate transfers, parole board hearings, and in the box for the following day, Hamlin Rankin's name and inmate number were written in block letters followed by L.I. Lethal Injection. Someone had crudely drawn a noose around Rankin's name. It was the state's first execution in nearly twenty years. They'd been prepping for it all month.

"Where am I supposed to get this kind of food?"

Briggs shrugged his shoulders. "Fuck if I know. Just get the guy a basket of gizzards from up the road. He can request whatever the hell he wants. Don't mean he's going to get it. Sick fuck's just renting the food for a few hours anyway. Ain't that right, New Guy?" Briggs said and laughed.

On his way into the prison that morning, Collins had to inch his car through the group of protestors and their signs—one side damning Rankin to fiery Hell, and the other calling for clemency—and he wasn't looking forward to doing it again. But as he left the parking lot, all that remained were a couple of college kids sitting on coolers drinking beer. One raised his can to Collins as he passed.

Collins sat in one of the stalls of the drive-in chicken place and watched several pretty young waitresses roll by on their skates. He held Rankin's order against his steering wheel, but he hadn't pressed the red call button yet. He looked at the menu behind the cloudy Plexiglas, and he knew he could order some gizzards or livers or a mixed dinner, maybe even the RC, and be done with it. But instead he pulled out and drove down the main drag to Cliff's Bar and Grill.

Cliff's was a narrow corner building, and Collins parked his car in the alley behind. He didn't want to go in, but there wasn't anywhere else to get food. He could've driven the twenty-five minutes into the city, and though he could use the OT, he just wanted to get this over with. Inside, Cliff's couldn't have been more than twenty feet wide. Collins flagged down the waitress and explained who he was, and after a moment she led him past the thin Tuesday night collection of refinery workers, men who might've remembered his father. When a few heads at the bar turned, Collins wished he'd changed out of his uniform; he'd been told during his orientation that families of the incarcerated often moved to town, so it wasn't a good idea to be seen out in uniform. It was yet another hazard of the job. He ducked his head slightly as he followed the waitress. A ball game played on the small TV above the bar, but Collins couldn't tell who was playing. The men had already turned their attention back to the game by the time he passed.

The waitress pushed open the swinging doors to let Collins into the brightly lit kitchen and said, "Hey, Jerry. Man here needs to see you."

"Yeah, a minute," he said without turning from the fryer, and the waitress left.

Even from behind, Collins could tell the man had done time. He had that tension in his neck and way of carrying his shoulders. He might as well have still been wearing the bright orange DOC jumpsuit.

When the cook turned and saw Collins, he flinched. It was an involuntary reaction to the uniform, Collins knew, and nothing more. The fryer beeped, and the man pulled the basket out of the oil and shook it once before dumping the contents into a butcher paper–lined cardboard carton and setting it in the window. "Order," he shouted.

Collins started to explain who he was and why he was there, but instead he extended the sheet of paper with Rankin's order. "Can you do any of this?"

He saw the man quickly look him up and down as he reached for the paper. He took it and held Collins's eyes with his own until Collins looked away.

"Is this—"

"Just get as close as you can, huh?"

"All right," he said after a moment, "but not for you." He turned and clipped Rankin's order to the thin cable above the window that held the other tickets. "Now, get out of my kitchen."

When Collins sat at the end of the bar, the man next to him quickly glanced down at Collins's hip. Then he tipped his chin at Collins before looking back at the TV. The man's hands were on the bar, and Collins noticed that he was missing the index finger on his left hand, the skin at his first knuckle still red and swollen. The bartender came and asked if Collins wanted a drink. He probably could've gotten away with ordering a beer, but he asked for water instead. He tried to watch the game, but he couldn't concentrate on it, so he pretended to study the specials' menu printed up on card stock worn soft around the edges. After close to ten minutes, the cook came through the swinging doors carrying two Styrofoam to-go boxes, the order taped to the top box. He set them on the bar in front of Collins.

"Our strip special and a seafood basket: some fried shrimp, cal-amari, and catfish bites. Threw in a few extra hush puppies. Not what the dude wanted, but . . ."

Collins opened the top box, and the steak inside was thin and curling up at the edges and had thick veins of fat running through it. Collins nodded at the cook. "Thanks."

Collins took the check from his front shirt pocket. "This cover it?"

The cook looked at the check. "Nah, man. I ain't takin' that."

"It's for the food," Collins said, but the cook shook his head. "Look, this money's spent. It'll screw up the budget. You gotta take it." The cook stepped back and raised his hands. "I'll just leave it here, then," Collins said and dropped the check on the bar. The Styrofoam containers squeaked against each other when he grabbed them. As he turned the cook stopped him.

"Wait." He picked up the check between his thumb and fore-finger like he would the tail of a dead rodent and jerked his head for Collins to follow him down the length of the bar to the cash register. The cook keyed in the order, and when the cash drawer opened, he slid the check beneath the tray. He tore off the receipt, but before he gave it to Collins, he pulled his billfold from his back pocket and took out a ten and a five and handed them to Collins.

"What're you doing?"

"The man's dinner's on me. And your fuckin' books are balanced."

Like earlier in the kitchen, he stared until Collins looked away, and as soon as he did, the cook walked the length of the bar and through the swinging doors. Collins picked up the food and the receipt and thought about leaving the money, but he grabbed the two bills, stuffing them in his pants pocket.

On his way back to the prison, Collins pulled into the Casey's. Like everything else on the prison side of town, it was run-down. The gas pumps were poorly lit and the sign was old—even the design was different from the new one out by the highway. Inside, he went straight for the cooler at the back and took down a bottle of RC and then made his way to the snack aisle. He couldn't find barbeque-flavored chips, so he pulled a bag of regular Guy's off the rack and took a King Size Reese's Peanut Butter Cup out of the bin at the front.

"That all for ya?" the older man behind the counter asked.

"Yessir," Collins said, and the man scanned each item and gave him the total. Collins took out his wallet and paid. While he was putting the bills in the register and counting out Collins's change, Collins noticed the rolls of scratch-off lottery tickets displayed in the plastic box to the right of the register. "Tell you what, I'll take some of those, too," he said and pointed to the tickets. He pulled the fifteen dollars out and put it on the counter. "However many this'll get me." Collins had never bought a lottery ticket and wasn't sure why he wanted these, except that they were right there and he had the money in his pocket.

"Depends. We got dollar ones, three-dollar ones, and five-dollar ones. Which do you want?"

"Pick me out the best. I don't care which."

"Okeydoke." The man took his time picking the lottery tickets before ringing Collins up. He put the food into a bag and placed the small stack of scratch-offs next to it. "A lot of people scratch those off here," he said. "That way, you get a winner, you just cash it in."

"Thanks, but I'm gonna hang on to them for now. You have a good night."

Back at the prison, Collins clocked out before sitting at the table and opening the food containers. The fat and juices from the steak had begun to congeal in the corners of the Styrofoam box, and the condensation from inside the container of seafood had turned some of the breading white and mushy-looking. Though he knew the guard who checked the food for contraband would probably pocket them, Collins took the lottery tickets from the shirt pocket of his uniform and divided them between the two containers, sticking half under a handful of fried seafood and the other half under the steak. Collins liked the idea of Rankin finding the tickets mid-bite and then somehow squirreling them away only to bring them out later in the darkness of his cell to test his luck one last time.

CHASING A LEAK

Most nights, at least those in the year since she fell at work and hurt her back, Crystal would take only as many pills as she needed to function, to keep the pain manageable, but two weeks ago Don had come home late from working a double and found her passed out on the couch. For a moment he wondered if she was dead, but then she snorted and shifted in her sleep. When he went to check on Jeffery and he wasn't in his bed, Don searched all over the house, finally finding him huddled in his tiny closet, so scared he'd soiled his pants and had been sitting in it all night. He thought he was in trouble because Mommy wouldn't wake up. After cleaning Jeffery, Don packed a duffel bag with clothes and other essentials and gathered as many of Jeffery's things as he could, but he only got as far as his truck. He couldn't leave. He didn't know how he'd manage work and Jeffery, and besides, he knew that while Crystal wasn't going to win any parenting awards, she was Jeffery's mother, and she was just trying to deal with the pain—Don had seen the X-rays of the discs in her back, it wasn't as if she were faking it. And, since his name wasn't on the birth certificate, he didn't have any legal recourse. If he took Jeffery, it'd be kidnapping; if he notified social services, they'd take Jeffery from Crystal and Don wouldn't have any say in where he ended up.

Things were better after that night. Crystal went off the Percocet entirely, sticking to extra-strength Tylenol and the exercises her doctor prescribed. Don knew that Crystal realized what she'd done, what could've happened to Jeffery, and she made a real effort to change. And for the past two weeks, she had. The exercises seemed to be working, and Don was optimistic that Crystal could go back to work soon and they could start getting caught up.

That was until earlier tonight.

He thought he heard it in her voice when he called to tell her he was working another double. "Where's Jeffery?" he demanded.

"Relax, baby, he's asleep. Tucked him in two hours ago," she said.

He'd been cut loose early in the shift, and as soon as he came in the door and saw Crystal, he didn't even have to ask. He'd seen her loaded enough to know. In the past they'd both dabbled in speed and other pills recreationally, but Don was always able to keep it together. He stopped, though, after Crystal hurt her back and started abusing the pain meds.

She weaved across the room to Don, wearing only an oversized Mickey Mouse T-shirt that barely covered her hips, the beer in the glass she carried sloshing over the rim and onto the carpet. She handed him the glass and kissed him, pressing her face too hard against his, sloppily jamming her dry and sour tongue in his mouth, her hands working at his belt and the zipper of his pants. She broke away from the kiss as hard as she'd initiated it and knelt in front of Don. She took him into her hand first, then her mouth. Her technique was similar to the way she'd kissed him, wild and sloppy. After a minute or two, Don grabbed her under her arms and tossed her onto the couch. He was rough with her, but he knew she wouldn't remember. If he couldn't punish her, or if he and Jeffery weren't enough to keep her clean, then he might as well enjoy it. And he did.

After he finished, Crystal stumbled down the hallway, and he heard the bedsprings groan where she flopped down. He sat on the couch flipping channels on the TV until he finished his beer.

Don stares at the ceiling, listening to the flat metallic pop of the water hitting the basin of the stainless steel kitchen sink. The sound carries through the small house into their bedroom, and Don counts to himself between each drip. It's hard to keep track with the noise of boxcars and engines coupling at the UP rail-yard a few blocks away. It never seems so loud as in the middle of the night.

Don looks at Crystal lying next to him in bed, mouth agape, snoring, sleeping it off. He imagines putting his arm around her, pulling her close, hearing her moan softly, and feeling her shift her hips to fit more closely up against him—but he doesn't move. He looks at the glowing red numbers on his alarm clock: 2:37. "Shit," he says softly and pulls back the covers and gets out of bed.

After slipping on a pair of jeans and a T-shirt and grabbing a pair of socks, Don leaves the tiny bedroom and closes the door behind him. The security lights from the salvage yard across the dead-end street cast a yellow glow through the thin living room curtains and down the hall, illuminating the crayon drawings covering Jeffery's door. Don cracks the door and looks in at him sleeping in his bed up against the wall, his little blond head poking out from under Transformer sheets. Don watches him sleep.

Not many people know Jeffery isn't his. Crystal didn't know she was pregnant until after she and Don had been dating for a month. When the doctor told her she was ten weeks along, it was clear the baby wasn't Don's. If you'd asked him a few months before he met Crystal if he'd ever date a woman who was pregnant with another man's baby, he would've laughed at the idea. But at the time, Don believed he loved Crystal, and he liked the idea of being a man who did the decent thing, the thing most men wouldn't do. Now, four years in, none of that seems to matter. He thought he was helping Crystal and Jeffery, but looking at their life—living on a dead-end street in Armourdale, a district in Kansas City, Kansas, named after a meatpacking plant—he's not sure what he's done to help, and he wonders how things might've turned out if he hadn't stayed. In his weaker moments, and they're coming so frequently now that he's not sure they're even moments anymore, Don thinks about leaving for work one afternoon and never coming back, forgetting he'd ever met Crystal, pretending none of it had ever happened. But he doesn't like to imagine Jeffery's future if he's not in it.

He gently closes the door and walks past the kitchen to the small living room.

Don sits on the couch in the dark and puts on his socks and work boots. Jeffery's toys are piled in a broken-down laundry basket in the corner of the room. At nearly three o'clock in the morning, it's one of the saddest things Don has ever seen. Even so, he knows he'll miss it if he leaves.

Taking his keys from the eye hook screwed into the plaster next to the door, Don quietly steps out onto the spongy porch. The smell of used oil and old grease hangs thick in the air. A car turns down the dead-end street, its headlights sweeping across the untended lot next to the house before coming to a stop and spotlighting Don. It's not unusual for SUVs with dark-tinted windows and large rims to come and go at all hours of the day and night at the back gate of the salvage yard. Though he doesn't know for sure what's going on, he can guess. Regardless, it's not his business.

Except for when it is, like the time he woke up in the middle of the night to find a burning car on the street. Don stands still, wondering if this will be the time someone gets out of the car. It doesn't take much for him to imagine a pretty, yet somber, news reporter standing in front of his house, the yellow police tape and lights behind her, and her thirty-second report of his murder.

Don slowly raises his hand to shield his eyes to get a good look at the vehicle, but the car turns and peels off, taking the corner at Cheyenne without even so much as tapping the brakes. Don walks the worn dirt path to the side of the house where his old extended-cab Dodge is parked. He opens the driver's door, and the hinges squeak loudly enough to get the dogs barking behind the eight-foot corrugated metal fence that wraps around the back of the salvage yard. "You bastards don't bark at cars or trains," he shouts at the dogs, which sets them off even more. He leans the seatback forward and takes the plastic Ace Hardware sack off the top of his duffel bag of clothes that has been in the truck for two weeks. He stares at the bag for a moment, then pulls it out. After the seatback falls and latches into place, he tosses it onto the passenger side floorboard.

Don lifts up on the sagging truck door and leans his hip against it to get it closed. He unlocks the large box mounted in the bed of the truck and from it takes a flashlight, clicking it to make sure it works, and the small toolbox with all of his hand tools and heads back toward the house, the new faucet rattling in its box as the sack bounces off his leg.

Inside, Don squints against the harsh light above the sink, and while his eyes adjust, he begins clearing several days' worth of dishes out of the drainer on the right. He puts away Jeffery's cereal bowl and several of the hard plastic plates, the ones from the mismatched set Crystal bought at a garage sale to get them by.

Don kneels on the dingy linoleum. The cheap veneer on the cabinet doors is warped and separating from years of damp dish towels hanging against it. He opens the doors, the dank and musty smell of wet wood and rot filing the small kitchen. After removing the assortment of junk that has accumulated—cleaning supplies, extra sponges, trash bags, dish soap, empty pickle jars set aside for cooking grease—Don turns on the flashlight and leans it against the bottom of the cabinet so the beam illuminates the space beneath the sink. He reaches up and turns the hot and cold shut-off valves before positioning the upper half of his body under the sink as best he can. When he turns over on his back, the particle board sags under his weight. The mildewy smell is stronger, and the sound of the last of the water still in the faucet dripping into the basin is much louder, like the slow pop of a snare drum. Don looks at the supply tube couplings and at the larger nuts that secure the faucet to the sink, reaches into his toolbox for a crescent wrench, adjusts the thumbscrew to fit, and begins disconnecting the faucet. The space is tight—Don hits his elbow on the inside of the cabinet on one side and the drainpipe on the other—but the supply tube couplings come apart easily. The two nuts holding the faucet to the sink are hard to reach, and with the way he has to hold the wrench, he smashes his pinky finger against the back of the cabinet a little bit on every quarter turn.

Though he's cramped and uncomfortable, he doesn't mind the work for what it is. At least there's progress. At UPS, where he's worked part-time since getting laid off at AWG, the boxes never stop. Work fast or slow, it doesn't make any difference because nothing changes. Boxes keep right on coming down the conveyor belts. AWG was a warehouse job, too—a good union job—but the work wasn't as oppressive. Sure, the food kept coming in and being packaged and distributed to grocery stores, but it felt different, more purposeful. But Don knows he's probably just romanticizing his old job because he can.

Despite the awkwardness of the space, the faucet comes apart more easily than he expected. It seems every time he's had to fix something in this house—even something simple like replacing a bad light switch—it's turned into a nightmare. It's like the house was cobbled together from spare parts and pieces. Though they are only renting, part of the agreement is that Don takes care of any repairs. They knew the place was a dump, but with Don laid off and the baby coming, they felt like they didn't have a choice. The landlord was a friend of a friend and the whole deal was a favor to Don and Crystal, but then he sold the property, and now they send the rent money to someone they've never met. Don wonders now who's doing the favor for whom.

Just as the second nut begins to spin freely, he hears footsteps in the hallway. The way the flashlight is shining, Don can barely see through the yellow glare.

"The hell are you doing?" Crystal's voice is gravelly and cold.

"I should ask the same."

"What? Can't hear you with your head under there."

"I'm replacing the faucet," Don says, a little louder. The nut is loose enough for Don to use his fingers, and after a few turns, he has it off.

"At three o'clock in the morning?"

Don scoots out from the cabinet. Everything outside of the halo of light over the sink is dark until his eyes adjust. "I was tired of listening to it drip."

"I hadn't really noticed."

Crystal's shirt is so faded and thin that Don can clearly see the outline of her breasts and where her nipples poke out behind Mickey's ears. It seems she doesn't know what to do with her hands; first they are on her hips, then she crosses them at her chest, and then finally she laces her fingers together in front of her. From the way she's slept, her hair is tangled and matted on the left side of her head, and on the right it hangs straight and stringy.

"Why you got your boots on?" she asks.

"Why not?" Don says and turns back to the faucet. Years of built-up dirt and grime have formed a seal between the faucet and the basin, and Don grabs the spigot and wiggles it. There is a soft plunk as it breaks loose, and Don pulls it out and places it in the sink.

"You couldn't just fix it?" Crystal asks, her voice warming slightly.

"The old guy I talked to at Ace said it's probably a bad O-ring somewhere on the stem, but for his money he'd just replace the whole thing. Said there wasn't much sense in chasing a leak. So . . ."

Don looks at Crystal looking at him. "You can go on back to bed."

"Maybe in a minute," she says and pulls out a kitchen chair.

Don goes back to work, quietly scraping with a putty knife the line of grit and corrosion built up around where the old faucet sat. He then takes the new faucet from the box and, lining up the gaskets, seats it on the basin. Without looking at Crystal, he takes the small plastic bag of hardware—new nuts, washers, and Teflon tape—that came with the new faucet and crawls back under the sink. As much as he wants to confront her about the pills, he doesn't want to hear any more of her excuses and promises, not because he isn't tired of them—he is—but because he's afraid he'll let himself believe her again. It's hard enough what he's thinking of doing, he doesn't need any other reasons to stay.

"Need these?" He leans his head around the light to see Crystal holding up the instructions.

"Just took one out. I'll manage," he says and goes back to tightening the nuts on the new faucet.

Crystal is quiet for several minutes, long enough that Don begins to wonder if she's fallen asleep or left the kitchen without his having heard. Then she says, "About earlier . . ."

He knows she wants him to interrupt her, to tell her it's okay, that he knows it was just a slip, the kind of thing he would normally say, but he's not going to give her that. Not tonight.

"Look, I'm trying. You *know* that."

"I don't know what I know anymore," he says, reattaching the hot and cold water lines.

Don gets up to make sure the faucet is seated squarely. As he kneels to crawl back under, he glances at Crystal. She has her shirt stretched over her knees, distorting Mickey, and she's leaning forward. She looks sincere, and he believes that she believes she's trying. But he knows no matter how much she says she wants to change, she's sick and it makes her selfish. He doesn't want to think about it because he knows he'll start to feel guilty, that if he leaves, he'll be just as selfish as Crystal, if not more so. 'Cause what is leaving if not a selfish act?

"You might as well head on to bed. There's nothing you can do here," he says.

"I'm sorry," Crystal says and stands, her shirt stretched out of shape and hanging crookedly off her shoulders.

"Me too." Don watches her walk down the hall and waits until the bedroom door clicks shut before moving. He reaches under the sink to open the water valves and hears the pipes moan slightly as the water surges. Standing at the sink, he raises the handle of the new faucet, and it hisses and sputters as the air comes out of the lines. As the water begins to flow normally, Don reaches back under and runs his fingers along the connections between the water lines and doesn't feel any drips.

He moves the handle between hot and cold, checking to make sure both work, then brings it back to the center but leaves the water running. He closes his eyes and listens to the shush of the water as it swirls down the drain.

THE CURRENT

From the canoe, Josh gazed at the rock bluffs high above him, and then across the river, a little over a hundred yards past the bank where the Ozark Mountains rose up out of the valley. He'd learned a few years ago in the fourth grade that the Grand Canyon was formed by the Colorado River, and he wondered if the Elk River had similarly carved its way through here and created this valley and these bluffs.

His legs were still wet from when he and his father had waded into the river, and the water tickled his fine hairs as it snaked its way down to his shoes. The river was clear and cool; in the shallow spots the multicolored rocks on the bottom formed a kind of mosaic, and Josh watched schools of minnows darting about before disappearing in the murky green of the deeper water. The sun warmed his back, and though the current was strong enough to pull the canoe forward, the resistance of the paddle in the water felt good in his hands and arms. And even if he was a little too short and the paddle a little too long, it hadn't taken him and his father long to find an easy rhythm that kept the canoe pointed downriver.

They'd put in with four others several miles upriver, but Josh and his father had fallen back, so they had this stretch of river to themselves. His father had told him how busy it could get on a Saturday and to expect more canoes and rafts farther along, but seeing it as it was now, Josh couldn't imagine it any other way.

"I'm glad your mother finally let you come down with me," his father said from the stern.

"I'm surprised she let me," Josh said.

Josh thought back to two nights before when his father had called to ask Josh along. *He's just a boy*, he'd heard his mother say into the phone. It stung, but he knew the truth of it—he'd just finished his first year of junior high. At school it was clear who were still boys and who were becoming men. It was the same with the girls. It seemed to happen randomly and without any warning to kids Josh knew in grade school, kids that he never expected to be anything other than what they were. Josh knew he wasn't alone; there were others like him, boys and girls both, but knowing and feeling were two different things entirely. He hoped his mother knew the trip was more than just getting to spend time with his father, something he didn't get to do much of, it was his chance, maybe, to stop being a boy. He hoped he could be one of the ones to grow up over the summer and surprise everyone at school in the fall.

After navigating the canoe successfully around the first bend in the river, his father said, "I know things have been tough on you, but—"

Josh turned on his seat to face his father. "It's okay." Actually, Josh thought, things hadn't really been difficult, or even all that different, but it seemed his father got some satisfaction out of these sorts of talks because he said something similar every time they were together.

"How's your mother doing?"

"She's good." His parents hadn't even been separated a year, and he was already getting sick of this question, whether it was coming from his father or someone else. It wasn't as if his mother and father didn't talk. In fact, they talked more separated than Josh ever remembered them talking while they were together.

"Is she . . . seeing anyone?"

Josh wasn't sure at first what his father meant by "seeing." "I don't think so, but Uncle Pete comes over sometimes." It wasn't until the words were out of his mouth that he realized what he'd said. He turned back and stared downriver, hoping his father hadn't heard him.

"How long's this been going on?" his father asked, and when Josh didn't answer, he banged his paddle against the top of the canoe. "Josh! Look at me. How long?"

Josh turned but couldn't look his father in the eye. One of the groups they'd put in with had stopped along the bank, and Josh watched them as he and his father floated by. "I don't know. He comes over sometimes and has dinner with us." Josh had never given much thought to his uncle's visits. He selfishly assumed his uncle was coming to see *him*, not his mother, but now he wasn't sure.

"How often?"

"Just sometimes."

"Sometimes. What does that mean?" his father asked.

"I—I don't know, just . . . sometimes."

"After dinner, does he stay?"

Josh shrugged his shoulders, hoping that would end this conversation, but he had heard his mother and his uncle laughing in the living room after he'd gone to his room to do his homework, and a few times even after he'd gone to bed.

"*Does. He. Stay.*" His father said each word in a harsh kind of whisper, like he'd pressed his lips tight so no one could see him speaking. Josh kept his eyes on the bank, looking at the people drinking beer, splashing in the water, and lying out on beach towels or in camping chairs. "Josh," his father said, his voice gone soft.

Josh looked his father in the eye and shook his head, but he knew his father could see past his lie. His uncle had stayed over at least once. Josh had gotten up in the middle of the night to go to the bathroom, and when he looked out his window, he saw his uncle's truck still parked outside. He understood now that he'd been too naïve to know what was really going on with his mother and his uncle. He'd foolishly believed his uncle when he said he stayed because he'd drunk too much. He thought about how dumb they must have thought he was. Josh wanted to punch himself. How had he not seen what was right in front of him?

"I'm sorry, Dad. I thought—"

"It's okay," he said. "I'm sorry, too. This isn't about you." Josh nodded his head slowly, but didn't say anything. After a minute or two his father said, "Hey," and took his paddle and hit the water to splash Josh. Josh didn't move, so his father did it again, soaking Josh's back. He looked at his father, and he was smiling. It looked forced, but even if his father was just pretending, it was better than the awkwardness from before. He hit the water again, and this time Josh used his paddle to splash his father back. By the time his father yelled, "Okay, okay! Truce!" the hull of the canoe was flooded with over an inch of water.

The cool water was refreshing, but in the slight breeze Josh got goose bumps down his arms and across his back. Behind him, he heard the cooler open and close followed by the crisp puff of air as his father opened a can of beer. They floated silently for close to half an hour, and the farther they floated the busier the river became. They approached a campground that was packed with campers and tents, and dozens of canoes had stopped on the rocky beach.

"Let's stop up here. Dump some of this water and get you some more sunscreen. Your mother'll never let you do this again if I bring you back sunburnt." Josh felt the canoe push left and looked back and saw his father dragging the paddle in the water. The current was swift in this section of the river, so Josh paddled hard on the right side to help get the canoe turned. Up ahead, he saw a cluster of four or five canoes bunched together along the rocks. A group of college-aged kids passed around a funnel with a long tube connected to it. One would pour beer in the funnel and another would put the tube in his mouth. Josh even saw a few of the girls do it. They were all laughing and shouting. Josh continued to paddle hard to get out of the current, and over the noise of the radio on the bank, he couldn't hear his father calling, "Whoa, whoa, whoa!" When they got to the calmer water near the bank, it was too late to slow down. Josh took his paddle out of the water and braced for the impact against the canoes. Even with his legs extended against the bow, he slid forward on his seat when they hit and glanced off. The canoes on the bank smashed together with an awful grating sound, and Josh heard one of the girls let out a small cry as the canoe she was standing next to slammed into her leg, knocking her to the ground.

One of the bigger college guys ran to the girl, but she was already giggling. The guy helped her up, then turned and stomped toward Josh and his father. "What the fuck, man?"

Josh turned on his seat. His father stood though the back of the canoe was still in the water. He raised his hands, palms up, in apology. "Sorry, fellas, we came in a little hot there."

"Yeah, no shit," the guy said. "You coulda really hurt my girl."

"Look, it was an accident. My son—this is his first time canoeing. Besides, she looks fine to me . . ."

"I'm sorry," Josh said, but no one seemed to hear.

"But it coulda broke her leg. If your kid can't handle a canoe, maybe y'all shouldn't be out here."

"I said I was sorry. It was an accident. No one got hurt."

"Not yet, anyway."

Josh saw the guy exchange a look with one of his buddies who'd come to stand next to him.

"C'mon, now," his father said, and Josh recognized the look on his father's face as one he'd seen once at an almost-fight while walking home from school. As he passed the elementary school playground a big kid was mocking and taunting a smaller boy, but when the smaller boy stepped up to fight, the bigger kid made excuses about not wanting to hurt the kid and how he'd only been "joking." The big kid had smiled then just like Josh's father now.

The college guy took two quick steps toward Josh's father, and Josh felt the canoe lurch. He looked back in time to see his father lose his balance and topple, arms splayed, into the shallow water. Swaying without the extra weight, Josh looked from his father on his back in the water to the college guy, who smirked and turned back to his friends who'd erupted in laughter. "Fuckin' old man," the college guy said, and someone gave him a high five as he went back to his group. Josh looked at his father on his back in the water, and seeing him that way made Josh's throat tighten. And for reasons he didn't understand, he couldn't get out of the canoe to help him, the same way he couldn't bring himself to sit with the overweight kid at school who always ate his lunch alone in the corner of the cafeteria.

His father stood without bothering to wipe the water from his face and got into the canoe. He didn't say anything, and he kept his eyes down, the water dripping from his hair, and worked his paddle against the river bottom to push the canoe off the bank. Facing downriver, Josh heard someone from the group on the bank say something about his father being a "bitch."

As they floated away, Josh didn't know what to say or do, so he sat quietly as long as he could. Behind him, he heard his father sniff and hock up a wad of spit before the lid of the cooler opened. The sound of his father opening a beer followed, and he turned and watched him chugging it. A beer or two was all he'd ever seen his father drink, and those times were rare. He'd even been a little surprised when his father brought beer on the trip, and when he loaded it into the truck, Josh had wondered if his father might even offer him one this weekend, though he didn't think that was going to happen now.

"Are you okay?" Josh asked, finally.

His father crumpled the freshly emptied can and dropped it, the aluminum clunking against the inside of the hull, and then he let loose a giant belch. Then he opened the cooler and dug out another beer, drinking this one as quickly as the last.

"Dad, are you okay?" Josh asked again after enduring several more minutes of floating in silence. The second can, like the first, ended up crumpled, floating at his father's feet.

"Josh, I'm sorry," he said quietly and paused. He stared across at the far bank. "You can't let . . ." He cleared his throat. "Josh, look at me, please."

Josh turned but avoided looking at his father.

"A man's got to stand up for himself, you hear me? Because if he doesn't, Josh, then no one else will. You understand me?"

Josh nodded.

They floated another mile or two, silent except for the sound of the cooler opening and closing. The skin on his neck and the tops of his shoulders felt tight, and he wanted to ask about sunscreen, but he didn't know how. Though his father's pace had slowed, Josh had counted at least six empty beer cans floating in the water at their feet. He'd never seen his father drunk before, so he didn't know what to expect or how to react. He worried about how he was going to deal with him if he got too drunk to get back to the cabin at the end of the float.

"I gotta piss," his father said. "Stop over there."

In his periphery, Josh saw his father pointing toward the large beach off to the right. This time the current wasn't as strong, and there were only two other canoes, so there was plenty of room for them to nose theirs up on the rocks. A group of four teenagers, three boys and a girl, stood at the water's edge. Josh didn't think they were much older than he was, maybe fourteen or fifteen, but the boys were drinking beer and the girl had a water bottle full of some rose-colored liquid. When Josh and his father beached their canoe, the girl waded out into the river and squatted so that the water was up over her hips, and Josh knew she was peeing. He'd already seen several women doing the same but never this close. Josh felt his face heat up; he didn't know why, but it embarrassed him that she'd do something so private right out in front of everyone. The girl, pretty, blond, and petite, wore a small yellow and white flower-printed bikini. She rose up out of the water giggling, and Josh couldn't help but stare as she ran a finger under the backside of her bikini bottom, pulling it away from her butt and letting it snap against her skin.

"Lay the blanket out and get the sandwiches ready for lunch. I want to rest here awhile. If you gotta take a leak, you can go when I get back," his father said and got out of the canoe and walked toward the tree line fifteen or twenty yards back from the water.

Josh did as he was told, spreading the blanket out over the rocks and getting the sandwiches from the cooler. He dug the bottle of sunscreen out of the bag, and while he spread some on his shoulders and the back of his neck, he kept an eye on the group of teenagers. They were making a lot of noise, and the boys were pushing and shoving and grabbing at each other, calling one another "Fucknuts" and "Dickwad." His gym teacher called it "playing grab-ass," and despite the name, it looked fun. Josh heard one of the boys say, "You're gonna get it!" and the girl squealed playfully and took off running. The boy gave chase and the girl ran right at Josh. For a moment, kneeling there on the blanket, Josh thought she was running toward him so that he could protect her. He started to stand as she got near, but she ran right past him, scampering over the corner of the blanket. The boy followed close behind, and Josh tried to reach for the food, but the boy shouted, "Look out, kid!"

and he trampled across the blanket, smashing the sandwiches. Josh sat and looked at the wet and muddy footprints and the mess that was their lunch. The boy finally caught the girl, scooped her up on his shoulder, and carried her out into the river. Josh watched as he tossed her in, and the other two boys joined them as they splashed and wrestled in the water.

"What the hell happened here?" his father said when he got back.

He gestured to the kids in the river. "They ran across it."

"Where were you?"

"Here," he mumbled.

"You just let them—goddammit, Josh! You can't—" His father stomped toward the river. "Hey!" he shouted. None of the boys seemed to be paying attention because they continued to rough-house, splashing and trying to dunk each other's heads under the water.

"Hey!" his father shouted again, louder this time, and the three boys stopped splashing and looked at Josh's father. The girl pushed her wet hair back off her face with both hands and wiped the water from her eyes. Her hair stuck up oddly on top of her head, and to Josh she looked noticeably younger.

"Did you just run all over our stuff?"

"Relax, man," one the boys said. "We're just messin' around."

"No, you just destroyed our lunch. Now, come over here and clean it up."

Josh wanted to apologize, to say that he'd clean up the mess, anything to get his father to stop.

"*What*? No. You shouldn't have put your shit out in the middle like that."

"I'm not messing around. Get over here," he said and took a few steps into the water.

"Fuck you, man," said one of the other boys, but his voice faltered.

"What'd you say to me?" Josh's father said and lunged at the boy, grabbing him by the back of his neck.

Josh watched as the boy struggled against his father, grunting and wildly swinging his arms. His father, who had looked so small next to the college guys, now towered over the teenage boy. The other two boys and the girl stayed in the river, seemingly in shock, like Josh, over what his father was doing.

"What'd you say to me, you little shit? Huh? Fuck *me*? We'll see about that," Josh's father said as he dragged the boy, stumbling and splashing, out of the water. He took him to the blanket and shoved the boy's face down toward it, just as he'd done to Josh's dog when it peed on the floor. The girl had started to whine as she bounced up and down on her toes and shook her hands at her side, and Josh wondered if she was the boy's girlfriend. The other two boys looked at each other before they moved together toward his father who was still holding the boy's face down and yelling at him about the mess on the blanket. Just then one of the boys shoved Josh's father from behind, knocking him to the rocks. The boy on the ground scrambled away while the two other boys went after Josh's father, kicking at his sides and arms and legs as he tried to stand. Everything had happened so quickly, Josh hadn't even realized he'd screamed, "Dad!" until it was out of his mouth. He ran at the boys to shove them away, but as his father struggled to his feet he swung wildly and struck Josh. It was a glancing blow, but it clipped the side of Josh's nose and sent him sprawling to the ground. Josh blinked hard and the world blurred. He reached to wipe his eyes, and when his vision cleared some, he saw blood flowing from his nose onto his chest. His nose throbbed, and when he touched it, he felt something shift under the skin and heard a crunch inside his head.

Fighting the tears that kept coming to his eyes, Josh looked around and he saw that no one moved, including his father who stood in the center of the three boys, looking dumbfounded by what had just happened and listing from side to side as if he had suddenly become drunk.

Josh managed to stand, and with one hand cupped under his nose to catch the steadily dripping blood, he went to the canoe and got a towel. He rolled it as best he could with one hand and held it against his nose. He looked again at his father and saw him pitch forward unsteadily and, with both hands on his knees, vomit. As his father's mess splashed on the rocks at his feet, the boys jumped back. "Shit, man," one of them said. The girl ran to the boy who'd been on the ground and threw her arms around his neck. The other two boys gave Josh's heaving father a wide berth on their way back to their canoe, but the boy he'd dragged out of the river shoved him in the shoulder as he passed. It was as if his father were a felled tree, slowly tipping over and crashing onto the ground.

Josh looked at his father lying on the rocks, snot running from his nose, vomit and phlegm on his chin, and then turned back toward their canoe. He took the towel from his face to check the bleeding, and since it was no longer dripping, he tossed the towel into the hull of the canoe where it splashed in the water and set his father's empty beer cans clanking. Josh pulled the canoe around so it was parallel with the bank and sat in the stern. He slung his leg over the side to keep the canoe from floating away, and he waited without looking at the bank. After several minutes, his father stood and walked slowly toward the canoe. Though his father didn't make eye contact, when he got close, Josh could see that he'd been crying, and before he got in, Josh reached down into the hull and grabbed the wet and bloody towel he'd used on his nose and handed it to his father. "For your face."

His father took the towel and slumped forward on the seat in the bow. Josh pushed off with his foot and paddled the canoe to the middle of the river and into the current.

DE FACTO ROMANCE

When he woke, he first smelled the strong aroma of coffee, followed by a faint whiff of urine coming off the stiff, musty couch. He turned slightly and felt the front of his jeans and was happy the smell wasn't from him this time. He couldn't really move to see where he'd ended up—his right arm, which was stuck beneath his body, was dead asleep.

There's coffee ready in here, a voice called.

Through the doorway of the kitchen, a woman sat at a table behind a haze of cigarette smoke, her pink bathrobe loose around her waist, a fluffy white cat at her feet. From his angle and the way she was sitting with her knees spread, he could see she wasn't wearing anything underneath her robe. He didn't recognize the woman, and after looking around the living room as much as his stiff neck would allow, he didn't recognize the house either. This wasn't an unusual feeling for him; he'd woken up in a dozen or more strangers' homes in town—few residents locked their doors at night. He'd close down Dusty's Tavern and stumble home only to find that he'd somehow ended up in someone else's house— affectionately called "pulling a Dale" by the guys at the bar. He'd been awakened by screaming women, run out by men wielding Louisville Sluggers, poked by children awake before their parents, both licked and bit by dogs, but this woman offering him coffee— that was new.

So as not to offend his host, he managed to roll his body off the couch and onto the floor. He struggled first to his hands and knees and then slowly, using the arm of the couch for support, to his feet. The room swung, like he was standing on a pendulum, so he closed his eyes and took a deep breath before opening them, and using various pieces of what had to be thrift store furniture—a beige threadbare recliner, a dinged-up end table, and finally an oversized china cabinet full of meticulously arranged baby angel figurines—he staggered his way to the kitchen. Though the pattern on the faded linoleum didn't help his dizziness or the headache sizzling behind his eyes, by the time he got to the kitchen, the world had stopped swinging and he could stand on his own. Dale recognized the style of the fixtures in the kitchen as the same that were in the house he grew up in. The cabinets, too.

The woman motioned toward the place at the small table where a Village Inn mug full of coffee sat steaming. Said, Sorry about you sleeping on the couch.

It's okay, Dale said, but he didn't understand what she meant. He sat and started to bring the coffee to his mouth when he noticed a large chip in the lip, so he turned the mug and took a long swallow. The coffee burned through the fuzzy feeling on his tongue. He looked at the woman and thought she had what people around here probably called a pretty face. The women in this town, the ones that stayed, either got hard around the edges, or soft. This one, whoever she was, had gotten soft.

Would of let you stay in bed, but when I got up to clean myself, she said and took a drag of her cigarette, you must've slipped out of bed 'cause when I come back you were gone. Found you on the couch sawing logs. Already had your clothes back on.

He took another drink of his coffee. Sorry 'bout that, he said.

He wondered why the woman thought they'd had sex. Did she have proof—a used condom? a stained sheet? That seemed odd and unlikely. And why would he put his clothes back on and then sleep on the couch? His thoughts were murky, but was it possible she'd fucked some mystery man who escaped out the back door just as Dale came in the front? Dale remembered leaving the bar, and he knew this woman wasn't with him then. He couldn't have met her between there and here, wherever here was, because he'd taken the alley in the direction he thought was home. Looking at this woman, he wasn't ashamed; sure, as drunk as he'd been, he *would've* slept with her, only he didn't believe he had. There was a woman or two he *wished* he could've forgotten he'd slept with, but she wasn't one of them.

You alright, she said. Look a little green at the gills. Here, she said and pushed away from the table and went to the fridge and pulled out a bottle of Seagram's. Her robe had opened at the neck, and Dale saw most of her heavy right breast when she sat. She either didn't notice or didn't care, just twisted off the cap and brought his coffee back to full. A little hair of the dog, she said and splashed a healthy dose into her own mug before placing the bottle on the table between them.

Dale drank, and the spiked coffee churned in his stomach but tasted good.

There you go, Sugar, she said and gave Dale the kind of satisfied smile he hadn't seen in years, since probably back when his mother was still alive.

For whatever reason, this woman thought they'd slept together last night, and though as far as Dale knew they hadn't, seeing that look on her face, he couldn't bring himself to say anything.

What's for breakfast, he asked.

Oh, Honey, I bet you're hungry after last night. What'll you want Miss Rhoda to make you? Scrambled eggs? Pancakes?

Pancakes'd be great, Rhoda, he said and leaned back in his chair.

CASHING IN

Each weekday morning *Central Standard* enters the different worlds of Kansas City. Regular topics include business, personal finance, the environment, information technology, education, music, and the arts.

KCUR—Kansas City Public Media
Part of the NPR digital network

Business correspondent Sheila Roland and a few listeners have a spirited discussion with Devon Jennings, founder of ProMourn, a local entrepreneur who's making waves.

"Cashing In" originally aired July 25, 2014. To listen to the full story, click *here*.

Sheila: I'm speaking today with Devon Jennings, founder of ProMourn, an unusual local start-up. Join our conversation live by calling 816-555-KCUR, or email your questions and comments to centralstandard@npr.org. Find us on Facebook or tweet us @CentralStandard. We'd love to hear from you. Welcome to *Central Standard*, Devon.

Devon: Glad to be here, Sheila.

Sheila: So, for listeners who might not be familiar with Pro-Mourn, start by telling us what it is and how the business came to be.

Devon: Well, Sheila, it all started about three years ago when my grandfather passed away. I didn't know him—he'd abandoned my mother when she was very young—so I wasn't affected emotionally by his death, and neither was my mother, really. The few memories she had of him weren't good ones. He drank and was verbally abusive. But at the visitation before his funeral, no one, aside from my mother, father, and me, showed up. For the first twenty minutes or so, the three of us stood next to the casket waiting to receive any mourners, and after an hour we'd gravitated to the first row of chairs. The funeral director approached my mother and asked if she wanted to continue the visitation for the remaining two hours, and my mother cracked. She cried like I'd never seen—sobbed, actually. My father and I helped her to the car, and she was so distraught she didn't attend the funeral the next day.

Sheila: That must've been very difficult . . .

Devon: To see my mother like that? Yes. Much later I realized that what she was probably feeling was a kind of fear and . . . embarrassment. As I'm sure you've experienced, funerals remind us of our mortality like nothing else can, and no one wants to believe that when they pass on not a single person will mourn their death.

But to return to your original question, I didn't consciously think about ProMourn until later. People of my age, their parents are aging, and a number of my friends' parents died over the course of a year or so, and I was going to more and more funerals. Most of the deceased I didn't know, or if I did, not well, so it was as if I were being invited to these funerals to in some way share the grief load, if you will. Like the more people who are there grieving, the grief gets spread out and somehow is easier to bear. Last year, as I thought back over all the funerals, it seemed there was a definite need, whether or not people realized it, for a service that provided professional mourners to attend visitations, funerals, and even the after-funeral luncheons. So ProMourn was born.

Sheila: Wait, professional mourners?

Devon: Yes. Our mourners are trained—highly trained—in grief and grief expression.

Sheila: So . . . they're acting?

Devon: Absolutely not, Sheila. Our mourners are totally present in the moment. They *are* mourning our clients' departed loved ones. Their training is an intensive eight-week course designed to prepare them for the job.

Sheila: You're listening to *Central Standard* on KCUR, 89.3, and I'm talking with Devon Jennings, founder of ProMourn. Devon, can you give us a sense of what the training entails? I mean, how does one go about preparing, as you say, for this kind of work?

Devon: I'm not comfortable giving the specifics of our training program—it's one-of-a-kind—but I will tell you that throughout the eight weeks, our mourners are exposed to countless hours of . . . well, death. Footage of the Holocaust. Nine-eleven. Katrina. The tsunamis in the South Pacific. Earthquakes and other disasters. Media coverage of school shootings and mass killings, both here and abroad. They're taught Affective Empathy—essentially they are trained to recognize and further develop our innate human capacity to empathize. There is also an element of Emotional Contagion, where they are trained to receive, or catch, the emotions of those around them. These are basic human functions, only we strive to heighten them in our mourners.

Sheila: I'm sorry, Devon, but this training sounds just awful. Why would anyone want to become a professional mourner?

Devon: Sheila, we're in a state of almost continuous mourning already. Are we not? There is death and destruction everywhere we turn. Our mourners are just people, like you and me, who decided to turn the grief they feel on a daily basis into something more positive. They can focus the overwhelming feelings they have on our clients' loved ones. For that moment at least, their grief is not anonymous as it tends to be in daily life. They tell me that it's honestly cathartic, and for some, it's even spiritual.

Sheila: So you haven't actually done it?

Devon: No. I leave that to the trained professionals.

Sheila: I see. Funerals are often steeped in religious tradition, so how does ProMourn handle that?

Devon: It depends on the client, Sheila. We cater to all faiths and denominations. Part of our mourners' training includes learning all the major world religions' doctrines on death and the afterlife. They study the death customs and traditions of different cultures and faiths. So, while our mourners aren't experts, per se, they can take part in nearly all religious funeral ceremonies. And we're working to hire mourners of every faith to better serve a diverse population. We've got Christians and Jews, agnostics and atheists, a small number of Muslims and Hindus. We even have a practicing Wiccan . . . and we're actively seeking Mormon and Jehovah's Witnesses mourners.

Sheila: We'd love to hear from our listeners. Call us at 816-555-KCUR or message us on Facebook or Twitter. So, Devon, who exactly are your clients?

Devon: The simple answer is they are individuals who have suffered the loss of a loved one and have a desire for others to mourn with them. But I think what you're really asking is why would someone pay for people to mourn for and with them? Am I right?

Sheila: Yes, especially with the rising costs of funerals.

Devon: For the reasons I mentioned before. Everyone wants to think people will mourn them when they die. In fact, we've started a service where people dictate in their wills what tier of service they want ProMourn to provide. We even have installment plans. Very similar to paying off burial plots while still living.

Sheila: Tiers of service?

Devon: Yes, we provide mourners at every price point. We recently did a funeral for a former celebrity who had fallen out of the limelight in her later years and wanted her funeral to be attended as it would have been during her heyday. As a way to kind of cement her legacy, so to speak.

We also do small, intimate services. And we just started providing free mourning services for indigents and people who have no family to mourn them. We believe it's important to mourn the loss of life, regardless of who the person was.

Sheila: We've got an e-mail here from Brenda in Tonganoxie, and she writes: "I was listening and had to speak up. I had a similar situation in my family. My husband's father was just like your guest's grandfather, and so few people showed up to his funeral. It was mortifying. I could see it on the faces of the few people who came. They were embarrassed for my husband. I felt so sorry for him—my husband." She goes on to say at the end, "Please tell your guest that had we known about his company at the time, we probably would've used it."

Devon: Thank you, Brenda. I'm sorry to hear of your experience, though it exemplifies one role ProMourn can play.

Sheila: We've got Frank in KCK on the line. Frank?

Caller: Yeah, uh, I've never called into the radio before, but this clown you got on there now? I couldn't not call. This guy should be ashamed of himself. He's full of [expletive removed]—I mean crap. Sorry! Taking advantage of people like he does. It's sick. I just had to say it. Thanks.

Sheila: Thanks for your call, Frank. And remember, callers, we're live on the air here.

Devon: Sheila, if I may? I'd just like to say to Frank, and to anyone listening, that ProMourn isn't taking advantage of anyone. We provide a service that people can choose to use or not use. We aren't forcing people to do anything. It's not as if some salesperson is knocking on doors, here. I just want to get the message out about ProMourn and what we offer. That's all.

Sheila: But aren't you, at the very least, cashing in on people's deaths?

Devon: Cashing in? I certainly wouldn't put it that crudely, but okay . . . who isn't? Pick a safety innovation of the last hundred years—seat belts? Safety glass? Car seats? Life jackets? Elevator brakes? Are the developers of those devices and systems not cashing in on death? What about crime scene cleanup crews? Or homicide detectives? Organ donor services? What about the various ways politicians cash in on national tragedies? Not to even mention the whole funeral services industry. Should I go on?

Sheila: That's not necessary.

Devon: Look, no one likes to think about it, but death is an industry. I'm not cashing in any more than anyone else, even this radio program for that matter, for doing this interview. ProMourn is a service, just like any other. If a person thinks they might be interested, then he or she should check us out. I think what we do is good and necessary, perhaps now more than ever given our increasingly virtual world. This is about people sharing something real and true . . . something . . . human.

Sheila: We've got another caller, Hailey from Overland Park. Hailey, welcome to the show.

Caller: Yeah, hi, in light of the recent tornadoes in Louisburg, I find it incredibly insensitive, shocking even, for Mr. Jennings to be hawking his so-called service and for the program itself for even airing this. It's opportunistic on both counts, and I'm disgusted by it. How do you sleep at night?

Devon: First off, let me just say how saddened I am by the devastation in Louisburg. Like you, my thoughts and prayers are with the citizens of that community, especially the families of those who died. Second, I understand where you're coming from, I really do. But I'm not swooping into town trying to sign people up for our service. I'm not flaunting my business in their faces. I wouldn't do that, particularly not at a time like this. We're not the NRA holding a rally after a mass shooting. That's not us.

And to your comment about me being opportunistic . . . well, as I said, if I am, it's no more than anyone else.

Caller: Of course it is. Here this tragic thing has happened, and you're on the radio advertising a service—and I use that term loosely—

Devon: I didn't tell the radio station that I wanted to schedule this interview right after one of the most destructive tornadoes in the history of the region. If I could predict that, I'd be in a different business. Are you going to rail against the construction workers and contractors that make money rebuilding houses and buildings in Louisburg? By your logic I suppose they should work for free? What about when some company donates to the cause? You don't think, as much as what they are doing might help, that they're still not looking out for their bottom line? If Hy-Vee donates a bunch of food and water to the relief effort, do you not see how that's free advertisement, not to mention a tax write-off, for them? How people might choose to shop at Hy-Vee over, say, Price Chopper based on Hy-Vee's humanitarian efforts? I'm sorry, but it's naïve to think otherwise.

Caller: But a grocery store donating food and water isn't as blatantly opportunistic as what you're doing. I'm sorry, it just isn't.

Devon: If you are inclined to see it that way, then I'm not going to change your mind. I'm sorry my company is being perceived that way because it certainly isn't our intent.

Sheila: Thank you for the call, Hailey. We appreciate it. I do want to reiterate, though, that we at *Central Standard* would never intentionally do something to offend our listeners. The stories and interviews we air are generally planned and scheduled far in advance. As Devon mentioned, we certainly didn't plan on this interview in any way coinciding with some tragic event.

We've got another caller, Jacqueline from Lee's Summit. Welcome to the show, Jacqueline.

Caller: Hi, Sheila, thanks for taking my call. I just had a comment for your guest . . . he said a moment ago something about how we are in a state of continual grief, or something like that? Well, I disagree. I don't mean to sound like I'm unaffected by what's going on in the world or anything, especially the local tragedies, but I consider myself a happy person, and I think it just comes down to how you see the world and choosing to look on the bright side of things. And there's already so much ugliness in the world, I think focusing on the positive is just good for everyone. Just wanted to throw that out there. Thanks!

Devon: With all due respect to the caller, what she calls looking on the bright side I call not paying attention or simply ignoring what's around you. But she's not alone in her views. In fact, I'm sure she's securely in the majority on this. And she's not wrong, either. It's much easier to ignore or choose to look on the bright side when death and awfulness surround us. It's a coping mechanism. It's difficult to function knowing the state the world's in. But I'd argue that ignoring it isn't the answer. So for truly empathetic people like my mourners, it gives them a chance to, as I said, turn the anonymous grief into something specific, and good things can come of that.

Sheila: So you're just doing some kind of favor for your mourners?

Devon: No, I didn't mean that. Only that the act of mourning our customers' lost loved ones connects our mourners to something communal and real. Real in a way that very little is real in today's world. And it's my belief, and the research bears this out, that communal mourning is a positive thing, psychologically speaking.

Sheila: Let's go to another caller. Ray's on the line. Ray, welcome to the show.

Caller: Yeah, uh, I was just flippin' channels on the dial and heard this. I'm actually working on a crew in Louisburg. A lot of us guys kinda migrate around, doin' this kind of work. We're not taking advantage of people. It's just a job, and if I didn't do it, somebody else would. So, this guy you're talking to? Seems it's no different to me.

Sheila: Thanks for that perspective, Ray. We've got our friend Clarence from Raytown on the line. Clarence, welcome back to the show.

Caller: I don't much get what this fella's sellin'. Funerals are for families and loved ones, not strangers. When my Margaret passed last year, I'd have been got-durn offended if some stranger showed up and tried to *share* my grief. But . . . the last I checked our country's still free and a man can do whatever he sees fit to make a livin' at. Didn't fight the Nazis for it to be any other way. That's all.

Sheila: Thanks, as always, Clarence. Nancy in Lenexa, welcome to *Central Standard*.

Caller: Hi. Thanks for taking my call. I've just got a quick comment for your guest, and I'll take the response off the air. Pardon my frankness, but ProMourn strikes me as you selling people on something they don't really need. Like, the service creates the need . . . Thanks.

Devon: Thanks for the comment, Nancy. I understand what you are saying, but isn't that the way of all modern innovation? We didn't know we needed the microwave oven until it was invented. The iPod? The smartphone? Special laundry detergent? Tooth-whitening strips? Organic food . . . the list goes on. Obviously, I think ProMourn is necessary in a way that an iPod, for example, isn't. I saw what I thought was a very real need in the funeral service industry, and I strove to fill it with ProMourn, and I think we've done a good job so far.

Sheila: You're listening to *Central Standard* on KCUR, 89.3. If you are just joining us, I'm talking with Devon Jennings, founder of ProMourn. I see we've got another email. This one is from Ed in North Kansas City. Ed writes: "Dear Sheila, I'm a big fan of the show. It gets at Kansas City in a way no other program does. Keep up the good work." Thanks, Ed. We think so, too. Ed's email continues, "I couldn't help but notice that your guest's business is, well, I don't mean to be rude or anything, but it strikes me as an extremely capitalistic venture. Especially given the recent destruction in Louisburg." Devon, do you have a response for Ed?

Devon: This is a business segment, is it not? Pardon me, but does Ed write in to say this to the person who opens yet another frozen yogurt or coffee shop? What about the man who runs a landscaping business? Do you ask him if the reason he's mowing lawns and trimming hedges is a capitalistic venture? My guess is you don't. Of course it's a capitalistic venture. I don't really want to harp on this, but since the caller brought it up, think about all the different businesses that will benefit, financially, in the rebuilding efforts in Louisburg in the coming months. Every step along the way, money is being made. From the demo and cleanup crews to all the different contractors: plumbers, electricians, drywall crews, painters, masons, and on and on. Is the town going to get rebuilt better and stronger? Absolutely. But it's not going to be free.

Sheila: We've got time for one more call. Uh . . . let's see . . . Chris out in Gardner. Chris, welcome to the program.

Caller: Hi, thanks for taking the call. I'm pretty fascinated by this guy's idea, though I'm curious, what does a person get for their money? You mentioned tiers of service, can you say a bit more about it?

Devon: Sure, Chris. For a specific breakdown of our services and the costs, I'd direct you to our website, www.ProMourn.com. But I can give you a general sense now. First, if there's time, say a person or their family has contacted us pre-death, we do what we can, and what the family or client allows, to get to know the person and their loved ones. We pride ourselves on our mourners' abilities to actually connect with the grieving family and to not simply anonymously grieve. It's in the connecting that real mourning happens. If there isn't as much time and we are contacted post-death, we ask several of the loved ones to fill out a short but thorough questionnaire about the deceased.

Sheila: That's all the time we have for today. I'd like to thank all our listeners and anyone who called into today's show—

Devon: Excuse me, Sheila? Can I just say one more thing with regard to the Louisburg tragedy?

Sheila: Sure, Devon. Go right ahead.

Devon: For the record, ProMourn sent a number of mourners to work the many funerals and remembrances in Louisburg following the tornadoes, free of charge and without, until now, anyone knowing.

But that's not the point I want to make here. Look at the outpouring of support for that community. I mean, all across Kansas City—and the region at large—people have come together and not only donated time and money to search and rescue and clean up but have shared in that community's grief. We came together in a way that rarely happens in this city, except for when something truly awful occurs, like the Louisburg tornadoes. Or back in '88 when those firemen were killed in that construction site explosion. Or the floods in '93. Or the way the city rallied itself around finding the identity of Precious Doe. Or our outrage in the wake of the recent shootings at the Jewish Center in Overland Park. And nationally, with nine-eleven and Katrina . . . in the wake of tragedy we come together and share our grief. We mourn communally, and it helps. It really does. That's all we're trying to do at ProMourn. Help people.

Sheila: Thank you for visiting with us, Devon.

Devon: Sheila, thanks for the time. I would like to add, if I may, that if any of your listeners are interested in purchasing a ProMourn service, if they mention this interview we'll take 15 percent off the price.

Sheila: And where can listeners find out more about your services?

Devon: Log on to ProMourn.com.

Sheila: Very good. Thank you, Devon. For more information about the people and places featured this week on *Central Standard*, please check us out at www.kcur.org. Thank you for listening. I'm Sheila Roland, we hope you join us tomorrow.

COMMENTS (3)

KAREN SHEPARD *07/25/2014 at 5:13 pm*

I tried to call during the show, but I couldn't get through. I just wanted to say we used ProMourn for a recent death in our family, and Devon's team of mourners were all we could have asked for. The mourners were so respectful and courteous, and . . . present at the funeral, I soon forgot that they weren't a part of our family and that we had paid for them to be there. I highly recommend ProMourn.

↩ Reply

DEVON *07/25/2014 at 8:03 pm*

Karen,

Thanks for the comment! I'm sorry your call didn't go through. There were so many callers that didn't get on the show, and I'm sure more than a few were former clients such as yourself trying to give positive testimonials for ProMourn's services. It would have been great to get your story on the air.

↩ Reply

ANONYMOUS *08/10/2014 at 9:19 pm*

SUFFERING FROM ERECTILE DISFUNCTION?? NO MORE! SIMPLY GO TO WWW.FREEVIAGRAFORLIFE.COM AND SIGN UP TODAY!!!

↩ Reply

PASTEURIZATION

Fifty-odd miles northwest of Kansas City, a four-door sedan—it could be light gray, or silver, or beige, a color you wouldn't be able to recall, and that's the point—winds its way down a gravel road. It follows the draws between the hills and crosses over several small creeks. The car hasn't passed a house in miles, and in the fading daylight, it turns under the arched sign announcing the entrance to the Wilson Family Dairy. On the rise a couple hundred yards ahead sits a white farmhouse and a cluster of large barns.

On a pole in front of the two-story farmhouse, a dusk to dawn light snaps on, illuminating little in the not-yet-darkness. When the car gets close to the house, a broad-shouldered woman steps out the door and off the wraparound porch and walks around to the east side down a short hill toward one of the barns. The car halts abruptly and the gravel crunches under the tires. The woman stops and looks over her shoulder. Her hair is twisted up in a knot at the back of her head, and she's wearing a large blue flannel shirt with the sleeves rolled to the middle of her ropy forearms. She looks at the car as if she's sizing it up, and then jerks her chin the way a man might and resumes walking. She stays in the middle of the little drive, and the car follows, creeping behind, its bumper only a few feet from her, but she doesn't speed up or step aside. When she gets to the front of the barn, she points to her left, and the car pulls around the corner and parks next to an old tractor with a large plastic tank on the back.

When the driver gets out, he is, like his car, nondescript. His hair is brown, or maybe dirty blond, it's not easy to tell, and he's medium height and medium build—say five foot nine or ten and around 165 or 170 pounds. He is neither attractive nor ugly, and the way he's learned to control his facial expressions make his face even less remarkable. Even with his carefully chosen wardrobe of black pants, shirt, and coat, like the stranger you pass on a busy street, you forget him the moment you look away, and that's the point.

The air is thick with the smell of cow manure, but the tickly smell of the pasture grass and hay cuts through it, but only just. The man gives the place a quick once-over: the lights are on in all rooms in the lower level of the house; a gigantic cottonwood tree that has shed nearly all its leaves stands on the south side of the house, and rows of pine trees line the west and north sides, outlining a kind of perimeter; three small outbuildings sit, like moons in orbit around the large barn; and about a hundred feet away, a barbwire fence separates pasture from everything else. Behind the fence two cows—a Holstein and a Jersey—stand looking. The Jersey lows at the man, and he's surprised at how the sound carries.

At the door the man raises his hand to knock but instead lowers it and opens the door. Inside, under the surgically white fluorescent light, a single Holstein stands tethered to one of the stanchion bars, its head buried in a bucket, its teeth grinding the feed. Behind is a row of milking machines and tanks, stainless steel with clear hoses. The room is remarkably clean, and a trough cut into the center of the floor runs the length of the barn.

The man hasn't been this close to a cow since a county fair as a child, but even then it was different, mediated. Though he knows he shouldn't, he approaches the cow and places a hand on its side. The hair is stiff but velvety under his hand, and though he can't be sure, he thinks he feels the cow lean into his touch. The power inside the animal, how much her ribs flex with every breath, is magnetic.

"That one there's a descendant of one of the first Holsteins my granddaddy bought." The man turns, but not too quickly, at the sound of the woman's voice in the back of the room. When she comes out from behind the milking machines, her boot heels clicking on the concrete floor, the man lets his hand slide from the cow's side.

"Her blood," she says and approaches the cow and kneels, putting her forehead against the top of the cow's head, "her blood, like mine, is as old as this farm." She pauses. "But she's gone dry."

The man, unmoving, watches the woman.

"*She ain't producing, let her go,*" the woman says in a deeper voice and laughs humorlessly. "Daddy's spinnin' in his grave, sure."

The woman pats the cow and stands to face the man. "I know it's wrong, but like a lot of things, it just can't be helped." She squints her eyes slightly, the lines in the corners deepening. She is a striking woman. Pretty is too soft a word to describe her, so let's call her handsome instead. She is a handsome woman.

"So you're him?"

"Yes . . . ma'am."

"Ma'am?" She looks the man over. "Jesus, you're young. Or younger than I thought you'd be. And you look . . ."

"Don't believe everything you see on TV," he says.

After a moment, she says, "How's a person get to doing what you do?"

"Some things can't be helped, right?"

"Fair enough."

They stand quietly only a few feet apart, and the awkward silence is broken only by the incessant grinding of the cow's teeth in the feed bucket and her breath chuffing through her nose.

"I'm not a bad person," the woman says, finally.

"Good, bad, it doesn't much matter to me."

"This farm's been in my family for three generations," she says and steps away from the cow to pace the room. "My granddaddy started out with just two Holsteins and a couple acres. Everything by hand then, of course. Nothing like what I've got here." She tips her chin, gesturing to the room full of machines.

"Jerry, my first husband, and I met right here. No kidding. Well, it wasn't in this barn, but in the old one. He worked for Daddy. Kinda like a fairy tale, you know? Farmhand marries the farmer's daughter," she says and smiles. "Only I wasn't up in the house cooking the meals and doing the wash, I was right out here working alongside Daddy. This," she stops and turns to the man, "this isn't all mine just because I inherited it. It's mine because I worked it."

The man nods.

"Jerry and I were gonna grow old here just like Daddy and Momma, then pass everything off to our two boys when they were ready. But the good Lord, in his infinite *God*damn wisdom, decided to take Jerry from me." She goes to the cow again and nudges the feed bucket with the toe of her boot. "After, I was lonely. The boys were doing more work around here, and I took up with Brent. It was nice the first few years, I'll admit, something different. He did the books and even helped with some investments that grew the business. Got us certified organic and into some specialty grocers. But then last year he started his talk about selling out and moving to Florida or someplace. Even brought some potential buyers here without asking me. See, it was never about the work for him. All he saw were dollar signs."

"Why are you telling me all this? It's none of my business."

"'Cause I need to say it, and you're here, so you get to listen."

"Okay, but . . ."

"We've got *time*," she says. "Keep it in your pants." She steps away from the cow. "He filed for divorce a few months back. He wants out? Fine. I won't stand in his way. But he and his lawyer are saying he's owed half this farm due to the *work* he put in. My lawyer says they might even have a case. Half this farm," she says again and takes several steps toward the man, her eyes wide and shiny in the sterile light. "I can't allow it. I won't."

It didn't seem right to the man, but she could've been making it all up and it wouldn't have changed a thing on his end. She's telling the truth, though, he knows.

"Now," she says after a moment, "this here's how it's going to go. Brent'll be here in a few. I told my lawyer I wanted to settle, but the only way I'd do it was if we could meet face-to-face. When he gets here, he'll probably want to be all business, that's Brent. I'll give you—ah, Jesus, I'm trying to tell you how to—hell."

"It's no problem."

The woman walks to the bank of switches by the door and kills the outside two rows of overhead lights, leaving the cow illuminated in the center of the room. The man looks around and, finding what he needs, disappears into the shadows in the corner on the same wall as the door. The woman goes to the cow in the center of the room and strokes its side.

Outside, the sound of tires on the gravel drive, a car door thudding, then silence. Two or three minutes pass, but neither of them moves. The woman stays fixed in the center of the room, directly under the only row of lights still on, and the man veiled in the darkness of the corner. Soon, boots on the gravel outside the door, the knob turning and the slightest displacement of the air inside the room as the door swings open.

"I been up at the house already. Should've known you'd be out here," the husband says and stops a few feet inside the door.

"Where else?" the woman says, but softly, like the rough edges of her voice have been sanded smooth.

"Late to be milking, isn't it?" he says and gestures to the cow tethered to the stanchion. "Somethin' wrong with her?"

"Dry."

"Oh. So, my lawyer says you want to settle?"

"I am," the woman says, and the man materializes, as if from the darkness itself, behind her husband, his gun raised to just behind her husband's ear. The sound of the gunshot and her husband's body crumpling under its own weight seem to happen simultaneously. The cow spooks, knocking aside the bucket of feed, snorting and thrashing against the rope, the metal clasp clanging against the stanchion in the silence following the gunshot. After a moment, it calms, then resigns itself to the spilled feed on the floor.

The man stands over the body, gun at his side. He looks at the woman. Her eyes are wide, perhaps in shock at how quickly—and easily—everything happened. He watches as she approaches and kneels next to her former husband. She rolls his body slightly and reaches into the front pocket of his pants, and it's as if she's performing some routine task. Her face betrays no emotion as she pulls his cell phone out, removes the battery, and replaces it in his pocket. She stands, steps a few feet away, and takes her own cell phone out and begins to make a call.

"What the fuck are you doing?" the man says. "Hang up the phone." He raises his gun at the woman.

Like a mother dealing with an impatient child, the woman raises a finger to the man, her lips pinched tight and her head cocked slightly.

"Hi, Ryan. Charlene. I'm sorry to call you at home like this. Probably interrupting your supper . . . You sure? . . . Well, goddamn Brent hasn't shown. I wanted to deal with him, but I can't if the sonofabitch . . . Yeah? . . . Okay. Let me know what you find out."

The man lowers his gun.

The woman nods. "Now," she says and walks to the cow. She uprights the overturned bucket of feed and goes to the back of the room where the light doesn't reach. When she returns, she's cradling a rifle in her arms, its stock shiny even in the low light. He can't tell for sure from across the room, but he guesses it's either a .30-06 or a .470. Winchester, probably, or Remington. The man trains his gun on the woman again, but she doesn't seem to notice.

Using the stock of her rifle on the ground as support, she squats at the cow's head and hugs it to her shoulder. The man circles left, like a prizefighter, only slowly. He stops when he's at her four o'clock.

"We're done here," she says without looking up from the cow. "Put your gun away."

"You first."

"I've got one more thing to do yet, so get on outta here."

"I'm not walking out that door while you've got a gun in your hand." The man knows he could kill her where she stands and to anybody that counted it would look like a strange murder/suicide. And it wouldn't matter to him, anyway, how it looked. But he'd been paid to kill the man, not her.

"Suit yourself," she says and turns to the cow. "Okay, darlin', that'll be enough." She speaks softly to the cow and removes the rope from around its neck and slides the feed bucket behind her, out of its reach. The cow's long, gray-pink tongue licks the feed from its nose and looks at the woman.

Then, in one swift move, the woman shoulders the rifle and places the barrel between the cow's eyes. Before the man can move or say anything, she pulls the trigger. There is a cymbal-like echo off the metal walls of the barn. The cow's legs buckle and it falls in a heap. Blood runs from the hole in its forehead down its nose and onto the floor.

"The fuck?" the man says, though his words are probably lost in the ringing following the shot.

The woman stands over the cow and her body sags, like she's merely clothes hanging from a line, and she's speaking, only it's too soft to hear. She takes a deep breath, and her shoulders spread as she turns and ejects the shell, the hollow metal clinking on the cement floor.

She turns to the man. "I told you to leave," she says.

"What about—"

"We'll take care of everything," she says and stoops to pick up the spent shell and puts it in her back pocket. She walks across the room, leans the rifle against the wall, and opens the door for the man.

He pauses before he steps through. "You didn't even need me," he says.

"I know. Except I couldn't. It had to be somebody else, an outsider. I've got a farm to run, and I couldn't risk it."

The sound of a tractor downshifting carries from behind the barn.

"Easy now," she says and raises her hand to stop the man who has reached into his jacket. "It's just my sons." She watches the man holster his gun and survey the room. He looks confused somehow, or disappointed, but at this point he's no longer her concern.

The tractor pulls around the barn, the headlights swinging across them in the open door. She presses the garage door button and the door raises. The tractor backs several feet into the barn, its backhoe scoop caked in dirt, and the engine shudders to a stop. One boy sits in the driver's seat, and the other, a couple years younger but stout as a man, has followed behind on foot. Neither of them seems fazed by either the body of their stepfather lying on the floor or the stranger standing in the barn.

"You boys do as I asked?"

"Yes," the younger one says.

"Follow the measurements I gave?"

"Yes," the boy says from behind the wheel. "Even able to go a bit deeper."

"Good," she says. "Good boys. Now, let's get this finished."

The woman looks again at the man standing off to the side as if she'd forgotten he was still there. "This here's none of your god-damn business." She holds him in her gaze until finally he nods his head once and walks to his car.

At that, the boy on the tractor climbs down, and he and his brother approach their stepfather's body and, one grabbing under the dead man's arms and the other his feet, carry him out of the barn and around to the front of the tractor. They heave him, no different than a bale of hay, into the tractor's bucket, the steel ringing out a dull note. Without speaking, the woman retrieves a coiled, heavy nylon tow strap from inside the barn, and she slips one end over the backhoe's scoop and walks backward, unfurling it to the dead cow. She squats and wraps the cow's head in her arms and gingerly raises it as her sons slip the strap around the cow's neck. They feed both of the cow's front legs through. It takes some time, and as they work, she looks over her sons' shoulders and sees the car backing out and driving slowly away from the barn, its taillights two red dots in the darkness.

"Ma? We got it, Ma," the younger boy says.

"Oh," the woman says and looks down at the strap tucked under the cow's shoulders. She lays its head down gently and stands, her shirt covered in blood.

The older boy climbs back on the tractor, but before he starts the engine, he looks to his mother.

"Take it slow, and don't do nothin' till I get back there." She looks to her other son. "You make sure that strap stays on, hear? I'll be along shortly."

The older boy fires up the tractor. He pulls out slowly, dragging the cow, a smear of blood in its wake across the barn's floor, the younger boy dutifully walking alongside.

The woman watches the tractor and her boys until they're out of sight around the corner. As the sound of the tractor fades, a cow lows in the dark pasture. She inhales deeply and blows out, her breath just barely visible in the cooling air. She surveys her barn, the bloody streak from the cow and the spot from her husband a grotesque exclamation point on the floor, turns, and follows her sons into the darkness beyond the barn's light.

THROUGH THE GEARS

The phone rings in the kitchen. It seems lately every time it's some-one asking for money—the Fraternal Order of Police or some fire-fighter's fund, March of Dimes, St. Jude's—so I've stopped answer-ing it. But it's awfully early, even for them. And on a Sunday, too. They don't usually call back right away, so if it rings again I know someone must really want to talk to me. The phone stops and a minute later it starts up again. I get to it on the third ring.

"Walter?"

"Richard?" I can't remember the last time we spoke on the phone. Like me, Richard grew up on his family's ranch, and like me he's still a bachelor. There's only four miles between us, so there's never any need to use the phone. His voice sounds different, like he's struggling to speak.

"Dad. He's gone," Richard says.

"Where'd . . ." I start to ask, and then I understand what he means. "When?"

"Just now, twenty minutes ago. Had a heart attack. Or something."

"Where is he?" I ask, but realize immediately how stupid my question is.

"I moved him to the couch in the living room." Richard takes a deep breath, and when he exhales, it sounds like a tornado has passed through the receiver.

I'm pacing the linoleum, the phone cord uncoiling behind me, and I can't find anything to focus on.

"You need me?" I ask, before thinking through what I've offered.

"I have to . . ." he stops. "Yes."

"Okay. I'll—" The line goes dead before I can finish.

I slip on my old boots by the back door and go out, and though I know getting there quickly won't change anything, I rush down the stairs to my truck parked alongside the house. When I get behind the wheel, the McGraws' house, a dark speck on the rise opposite mine, is framed in the center of the passenger window. I start the truck and slip it into gear, and in moments I'm on the road, the gravel ticking and popping in the wheel wells. In the few minutes it takes to cross the valley, I think about Leonard for the first time since picking up the phone.

When I was fourteen, my own father died on the ranch. I found him impaled on the hay bale spear in the corner of the barn where I'd come to do my chores after school. His shirt was soaked dark red, and a muddy pool of coagulated blood had collected on the barn floor beneath him. He must've stumbled and fallen onto it because a box of tools was spilled across the floor. Later, I found the tractor broken down on the back eighty; I suppose he'd returned on foot for tools to try to fix it. The bale spear is still in the barn, and often when I pass it, I think of him struggling to lift himself off all afternoon and bleeding out there in the barn, my mother less than fifty yards away in the house.

I was old enough to take care of most everything, and though I made a lot of mistakes that first year, Leonard never once overstepped his bounds, out of respect for my father, and me.

I drive under the cedar archway gate at the head of the drive. Before I get out of the truck, I look down at my jeans, threadbare and holey, and at my worn work shirt. I don't usually think about my clothes, and for a moment I consider turning back to change into something more appropriate—but, then, what's appropriate for a time like this?

I hurry up the front walk but stop at the door—I haven't knocked or rung his doorbell since we were kids. I open the door quietly, though I don't know why, and step inside.

I've been coming to the McGraws' my whole life. I know this house and its outdated furniture and fixtures as well as my own, but it all looks different, empty somehow. I walk softly toward the living room, and if someone were watching, they'd surely think I was a burglar. When I turn the corner at the living room, I see Leonard lying on the couch, his head propped on a pillow as if napping, and Richard kneeling on the floor with his head on his father's chest. Richard doesn't move, so I stand in the doorway for close to a minute before I shuffle my feet slightly. "Walter," Richard says without raising his head, and I sit on the edge of the recliner across from the couch. Leonard's eyes are closed, but his mouth is open slightly and his chin is cocked to the side, and there's a large dark spot at the crotch of his pants.

"I have to make some calls. Can you stay with him?"

"I'm not going anywhere."

"Can you just hold his hand while I'm gone?" I don't answer right away, so he adds, "Please?"

Richard stands without looking at me, and I roll the ottoman to the couch and sit. When I take Leonard's large hand in mine,

Richard leaves the room. Leonard's hand is still warm and softer than I expect. As I hold his hand I'm reminded of the only time Leonard ever offered to help me. It wasn't long—only a month or two—after my father had died, when I tried to teach myself to drive Dad's old '56 Chevy pickup. Mom couldn't drive a stick shift, and we couldn't afford a new truck, so I tried to learn on my own. It took me several tries grinding the starter before I figured it out, and I stalled a dozen times or more before I even got to the road. I saw the tail of dust on the wind before I noticed Leonard's truck coming down the hill.

He pulled up beside me. "Need help?"

I nodded, but I didn't look him in the eye.

He pulled Dad's truck back to the house and told me to get behind the wheel of his. He quietly explained how to work the clutch and the gas, and he placed his large hand over the top of mine on the black gearshift knob and guided me into the correct gears. His truck was brand new, and I was scared of burning up the clutch or ruining the transmission. I stalled the truck over and over, but he never said a word about it, even as the smell of the burning clutch seeped into the cab. He just kept coaching me through the gears.

When Richard comes back into the room, he sits in the recliner across from the couch and asks me why I'm crying.

AS MUCH AS ONE DESERVES

See a lot of interesting things in my line of work. Some good: like earlier this spring when I showed up for a tow call and found a bride in her long white dress and the groom in his monkey suit standing next to the ditch where the bed of their bright red pickup poked up in the air, the long strings of beer cans dangling from the chrome bumper, the "Just Married" scrawled across the back glass barely visible at that angle.

Neither seemed upset; in fact, when the two of them climbed into the backseat of my rig after I got their truck pulled from the ditch and loaded on the wrecker, they couldn't keep their hands off each other. Before I knew it, in my rearview mirror I saw the gal working her dress up around her hips so she could straddle her new husband. I half wished my truck had one of those partitions between the front and rear to give them some privacy, but I kind of wished I didn't have to keep an eye on the road, too. It was something, those two. Here they just wrecked their truck leaving their wedding, but it didn't seem to bother them one bit. Hell, my ex and I would've been at each other's throats, even back when we were young and hot for each other. I'll bet the ol' boy lost control of his truck because his bride couldn't keep her hands off his zipper.

And then there's the bad: like the call I went on a few weeks ago.

There was nothing special about the way the workday started—a couple fender benders in the morning, an illegally parked towaway in Old Town around lunchtime, and a flat tire out on West Kellogg in the early afternoon—but then the call before the call I mean to tell you about came in. Ernesto, a cop friend of mine, sent me a text about a breakdown in Eastborough. Protocol is for Ernesto to call it in and for the dispatcher to then call for a tow truck, so Ernesto doesn't get in touch with me directly unless he thinks there's an opportunity. Plus, Ernesto's a Wichita cop. Eastborough is a little village in the middle of Wichita with its own city hall and police force (all of three cruisers), and its residents are in a tax bracket I couldn't reach with a rocket ship. Let's just say I'm surprised they don't have gates at the entrance. The people in Eastborough don't drive cars that break down, or at least that's what I thought until I saw the blue '69 Camaro sitting on the side of the road, a little steam still wisping out from under its hood.

Ernesto knew better than to stick around and was already gone when I pulled up. Before I could even get out of my truck, a kid, probably all of seventeen, comes to my door. He's got sunglasses on and he's wearing khaki shorts, a yellow golf shirt, and flip-flops. He starts right in on me.

"You're late, you know that? I've been waiting, like, ten minutes."

With that, I decided to take my time. Dug around in my console, made like I was looking in the backseat for something, studied a blank form on my clipboard.

"Look, *chief*, I'm not messing around here. I just might have to make a call to your supervisor."

It wasn't the threat of calling my boss, it was the "chief" that did it. I do my best not to get into it with people like this, but this kid pissed me off. People like him think people like me don't have anything better to do than sit around waiting for their phone call, like we need them or something. From the looks of things, this kid needed me a whole helluva lot more than I needed him.

I got out of the truck faster than he expected, and he took a couple steps back and looked me over. I could see he hadn't expected me to be so big or to move so quick. It seemed the long hair and Fu Manchu, tattoos, and shit-kicker boots made an impression on him. I still hadn't said anything.

After a moment of neither of us speaking, the kid took off his sunglasses and said, "The car, all of a sudden it just started smoking." He was scared. It was probably Daddy's and he wasn't supposed to have it out. I decided to give the kid a quick test.

"Pop the hood and I'll take a look," I said. The kid opened the driver's door and reached under the dash. His eyes got a little bigger when he didn't find a hood release lever. Here this kid was driving a classic, and he didn't even know how to open the goddamn hood. I stuck my fingers in the front grille, found the lever, and popped it.

When the kid came around the front, he asked, "Well?"

Lots of people assume tow truck drivers are mechanics, and I suppose some of them are, but I'm not. However, even I could see all that had happened was the lower radiator hose had split and the fan had thrown coolant onto the headers. As long as he'd shut it down soon enough, the engine would be fine. A little part of me felt good for the kid—he hadn't done any major damage to his dad's car—but a much larger part thought, Fuck this little shit for getting to drive this car, and fuck his dad for not teaching him anything about it. Probably didn't even know anything about it himself. So, when I leaned in over the engine, the brown sugary smell of the burnt antifreeze rising to my nose, I paused just long enough to sell it. "I don't know, buddy, it doesn't look good."

"Oh, shit," he said. "Can you fix it?"

"Me? Hell no. This kind of work is above my pay grade. I mean, if it were just a belt or a hose, then maybe, but what we're dealing with here looks to be internal."

"Fuck. You've got to help me out, man," he said, his voice breaking into a whine. "My dad can't know about this."

"I got a guy that might be able to take a look at it. He usually only works by appointment, but he owes me one . . ."

"Please, man, what's it going to take?"

Bingo.

"My guy owes me, but I don't want to just give that favor up for nothing." The kid took out his wallet and handed me a hundred-dollar bill quicker and easier than I had anticipated; it seemed he understood perfectly. If you had money, and he clearly did, you could buy your way out of just about anything. Who am I to disrupt this system? I thought about pushing it, seeing as how easily he forked over the hundred, but I wasn't done with him just yet. There was still some money to be made. I folded the bill and put it in my pocket. "Let's get you hooked up."

The kid was quiet on the drive to Duane's shop. Duane's actually a good mechanic, but like me, he's not above taking advantage when the situation presents itself. And this was one of those situations. Duane and I don't do this a lot, but we've done it enough times to develop a kind of system. I'm sure he knew it was on when he saw me pull in with the Camaro, but I gave him a quick nod in the garage just to be sure. I left while he was giving the kid his spiel. I didn't know how much Duane would be able to get out of the kid, but I knew it'd be a nice chunk of change, 30 percent of which was mine—my finder's fee. Even after kicking Ernesto a few bucks, I'd be in good shape.

I was riding pretty high leaving Duane's. A hundred dollars richer, and though I wasn't especially proud of screwing the kid over, I'd scored a few points for the working man. I was thinking about what I'd do with my extra hundred when *the* call, the one this story is really about, came in. I knew before I showed up that it probably wasn't going to be good because the dispatcher told me the highway patrolman that called it in said it was a multiple car accident. It happened north of town on 254, kinda out in the country. There's quite a bit of traffic out there, though—it runs between Wichita and El Dorado and lots of people take it to avoid the toll on the turnpike. It's a four-lane highway divided by a grassy median, but it's not an interstate so there aren't any exit ramps. Cars have to cross the opposite two lanes if they want to make a left turn down any of the side roads, and the speed limit is seventy. When accidents happen out here, they're bad.

On my way to the scene, while I weaved through the traffic that had backed up a good quarter mile, I heard the Life Flight helicopter before I saw it lifting off the ground.

One of those.

When I finally got through the traffic, I couldn't actually see anything because the ambulance and police cars, their cherries still burning, had blocked both eastbound lanes and one of the westbound ones. While I waited for an officer to clear a path around the blockade, I saw a man being loaded into the back of an ambulance. He was strapped to a backboard and his head was secured in a brace, and an EMT was walking alongside the stretcher, squeezing one of those bags to keep his oxygen flowing. The officer waved me around, and at the back of another ambulance, two emergency workers were loading two black body bags. With close to half a million people in and around Wichita, there are plenty of wrecks, but with the way the city is laid out and the few highways, there just aren't that many fatality accidents. This wasn't the first time I'd seen this kind of thing, but it wasn't something I'd grown used to, either. I don't know how the cops and EMTs deal with it. Then I came upon the wreck, or at least its aftermath. It takes a lot for a couple of wrecked cars to get my attention, but let me tell you, this was something. It was no wonder people died.

I saw what used to be two vehicles, one angled across the two eastbound lanes, and one off in the grass in the median. As I pulled around the front of the vehicle in the highway, I could tell it was an SUV, but it was too smashed for me to recognize the make. From the way it looked, no one inside could have survived. The front half was gone from the firewall forward—the engine was sitting out in the middle of the highway in a pool of oil and coolant—and the right side was hit so hard and had caved in so much that the driver's side doors must have jammed because the roof was peeled back on the passenger's side where the firemen had used the Jaws of Life. I got out of my rig to lower the flatbed and hook up the winch and saw the blue oval on the center cap on one of the rear wheels; I figured it to be a Ford Escape. It was too small to be an Explorer. But it didn't matter anymore; the scrap yard wasn't picky.

After I'd secured the winch hooks to the frame and started dragging the Escape up the flatbed, the screeching metal piercing the quiet of the accident scene, something flashed in the backseat area and caught my eye, and I released the lever to stop the winch. The front of the Escape was up on the flatbed but the rear wheels were still on the ground, so I didn't have to climb up to see inside. As I approached the hole in the rear door where the side glass used to be, the silver backside of a Mylar balloon turned in the breeze, and on the front, in bold blue letters, it said: "It's a Boy!" I leaned my head in; a car seat sat strapped in the center of the backseat and next to it a fuzzy, smiling blue bear with the string of the balloon tied around its paw. I'm a big man and I cast a pretty mean shadow, but I shit you not, it felt like my stomach dropped into my boots. I got light-headed and had to grab ahold of the door to keep my feet. Though I didn't want to, I looked in the back again. The belts on the car seat harness had been cut, and I thought about the Life Flight. I looked again at the smiling bear; the car was smashed all to hell, yet here in the backseat sat a stuffed bear and a balloon that hadn't been touched. How the balloon didn't pop, I'll never know.

I went through the motions of securing the Escape to the flatbed, trying to keep my shit together, and it wasn't until I saw another wrecker pull up to tow away the other vehicle—a four-door Silverado with the front end crushed in bad—that I remembered the man the EMTs were working on. Based on the damage to the two vehicles, if I'd had to guess, I'd have said the man was the driver of the truck. It looked more survivable, but he was still a lucky sonofabitch; at least the ambulance he was riding in had its lights on.

I double-checked to make sure the carcass of the Escape was secure before getting back in my rig. I weaved through the collection of police cars and emergency vehicles until my path cleared and the highway opened up before me. I headed back toward Wichita to the city impound lot, but I only made it a couple miles when I noticed in my upper side mirror the balloon dancing around in the back of the Escape. I flipped on my lights and pulled to the shoulder. In my mirror I watched as the balloon whipped around in the air as cars passed. It jerked against the string so hard when a semi roared by, I thought for sure the string would come loose from the bear and it would float away. When it was finally clear, I got out and hustled back to the flatbed and hauled myself up. I reached into the back of the Escape, careful not to cut myself, or the balloon, on the crumbles of safety glass, and took the bear and balloon out. I carried them up to the front and put them gently on the passenger side of the bench seat. After what that balloon had survived, I wouldn't have been able to stand seeing it pop now. Besides, the balloon and bear belonged to that little boy, and if he survived, then I meant to return them to him.

On my way back to the city lot to drop off the Escape, I got a call from the dispatcher to pick up a car in the Delano district, but I begged off. I told her I wasn't feeling well, and it wasn't a lie. With the A/C blowing full blast on the drive back, the balloon twisted and bobbed around the cab of the truck, almost playfully, like it understood its purpose, and there was that bear sitting next to me on the seat, still smiling as if nothing had happened. It got so I couldn't even look at it. I was half tempted to pull off somewhere and toss them in a Dumpster or down a storm drain, just to be rid of them, but I knew deep down I couldn't.

After unloading the Escape, I stopped off at F & K Liquor on the corner of Woodlawn and Lincoln just down the street from my house. After the day I'd had, a twelve-pack of High Life was in order.

I'd already finished one beer by the time I pulled into my driveway. I tucked the opened box of beer under my arm and got out. When I closed the door, the balloon shifted on the displaced air in the cab. I made it inside my house without looking over my shoulder. Inside, I put the beer in the fridge next to a couple stragglers that I would have normally drunk first, but they were microbrew that Ernesto had left the last time he was over, and I wanted to drink fast.

I took out another High Life and twisted off the top. After a long swallow, I had half the bottle finished. I sat on the couch and turned on the TV. I checked the four local news stations for coverage of the wreck, finishing my beer while jockeying between the channels. At the fridge getting a fresh one, I heard the anchorwoman say something about a wreck on 254. I hustled back into the living room, my new beer foaming over the lip of the bottle, just in time to see the stock accident footage—the road flares, the emergency vehicles, the backed-up traffic—and hear the off-screen reporter say: *". . . three fatalities, two adults declared dead on the scene, and an infant that died at the hospital. The driver of the other vehicle suffered life-threatening injuries. He's currently listed in critical condition at Wesley. Police speculate that alcohol may have played a role in the accident. Gina Thompsen reporting from highway 254 in north Sedgwick County . . ."* I muted the TV and walked away.

The third beer went down even faster than the first two as I paced the house. Before I knew it, I was standing at my living room window looking out at my truck. At first it looked like the balloon was still, but the longer I looked at it, I noticed it was turning ever so slightly like it couldn't help moving.

I drank two more beers standing at the window before I finally went outside. When I opened the passenger side door, it caused a kind of vacuum and sucked the balloon toward the open door. It strained against the bear's wrist. I gathered the bear in my arms and held the string tight. When I got inside, I set the bear, which was probably only slightly larger than the infant it was meant to celebrate, in the center of my kitchen table, and the balloon bobbed a few times before settling into a calm listing from side to side as I drank my way deeper into my twelve-pack.

It had gotten dark outside without my noticing, and I hadn't bothered to turn on any lights in the house. The TV was still on in the corner of the living room, projecting its flickering light against the wall in front of me. I looked at the bear and balloon and the shadows they cast on the wall. Then I saw my shadow, a dark, featureless mass. I reached for the bear and buried my face in its soft blue fur and inhaled deeply. Whatever I was trying to smell was gone.

I woke up at the table with my head on the bear as a pillow, the balloon floating above my head like a thought bubble in the funny papers. It was still early—I hadn't overslept—and my neck was pinched tight and my brain felt loose in my head. I made a pot of coffee after I took a shower, and while I was waiting for it to finish brewing, a police siren blipped outside my house, and I knew it was Ernesto. He stopped by for coffee every now and then at the start of his shift. When I met him at the door, he said, "So?"

"So, what?" I asked and stepped aside to let him in. Ernesto wasn't fat—stocky maybe—but at only five six on a good day, and with the uniform, Kevlar vest, and police belt, he was thick. It didn't help that all his gear squeaked when he walked.

"What do you mean 'so, what?' That kid yesterday with the Camaro. Was I right?"

After the night I'd had, I'd completely forgotten about that kid. "Yeah, you were right."

"Aha! Just leave it to the Mexican to sniff out the chump."

Ernesto is always saying shit like this, and it rarely makes any sense. He's Mexican, all right, dark skin, dark hair, dark eyes, the works. But even though he pronounces words like *tequila, guacamole,* and *jalapeño* with an accent, he doesn't speak a word of Spanish.

"So," Ernesto continued, "how much did we get him for?"

"Duane'll let me know the next couple days," I said and remembered the hundred the kid had given me. I probably should've split that with Ernesto, but money he didn't know about didn't really exist.

"I knew it the minute I saw that punk." The coffeemaker beeped in the kitchen and Ernesto gestured toward it and I nodded. "Shit, man, you have a party last night?" he asked and I remembered the beer bottles in the sink and the ones on the table. Before I could answer he said, "Who had a baby?"

I told Ernesto about the smashed-up SUV and the bodies and the baby seat, and how I'd seen the paramedics working on the driver of the other vehicle. Ernesto said he'd heard that call go out over the radio at the end of his shift. I explained to him how the bear and balloon were unharmed, how I couldn't just leave them in the vehicle, and how I'd planned to return them, but the baby died. "Damn," Ernesto said. "*Damn.*"

"I need you to look into this. Find out who the driver is." It wasn't until I said it that I realized I had to know more about the guy who'd been driving the truck. I needed to see what kind of man he was because it was clear I wasn't going to get over this anytime soon.

"You realize what you're asking me to do?"

This from the man who the day before helped me scam a rich kid, and who from time to time pockets the dime bags and half-smoked joints he confiscates from teenagers. I don't mean to make him out to be a bad guy—he's not—but I wasn't going to let him get high and mighty on me when I asked a favor of him.

"Yeah I do. I'm asking you to ask around, to punch some shit into a computer, whatever. And don't give me any shit about your 'job.'"

Ernesto finished his coffee in silence, and when he left he didn't say he'd look into the accident, but he didn't say he wouldn't, either. When I left for work I grabbed the bear and balloon off the table.

The two rode shotgun with me until I towed a woman and her car from Towne East mall to a mechanic downtown. When she climbed in the truck and saw the bear and balloon, she said, "Oh." When I brought them with me I hadn't thought about anyone riding along. I placed them as gently as I could in the backseat. "Who had a baby?" the woman asked.

"My sister," I said.

"Congrats, *Uncle*," she said. "Is this your first nephew?"

I nodded. "I'm going to the hospital after work."

"You'll have so much fun being an uncle. You get to spoil 'em, get 'em all riled up, and send 'em home to Mom and Dad." The woman laughed and went on to tell me all about her kids— she had three, two girls and a boy—and I did my best to act interested.

My ex and I had wanted kids, but hard as we tried we couldn't make it happen. We never went to the doctor or anything. I'm not even sure we knew there was such a thing as a fertility clinic back then. Couldn't have afforded it anyhow.

While I waited for the guy in the office of the mechanic's shop to sign for the woman's car, I got a text from Ernesto. *Glenn Murphy. BAC .19 1030 S. Capri Ln. Dont make me regret this.*

• • •

Early that afternoon after my last tow, I looked up Glenn Murphy's address on the GPS and was surprised to find he only lived a couple miles from me. I didn't know what to expect or what I was going to do when I got there, but I had to see where he lived. Though I hadn't given it much thought, for some reason I'd expected him to live in a neighborhood like mine—full of houses that were built as temporary McConnell Air Force barracks during World War II, but later sold and converted into low-rent fourplexes. I pulled into the neighborhood and couldn't believe how normal all the plain brick ranch houses looked, just like dozens of other postwar neighborhoods in Wichita. When I turned down Capri Lane and the GPS voice told me my destination was on the right, I slowed as I passed the house. In the driveway a tall, thin brunette woman and a small boy were getting out of a beige sedan. The woman said something to the boy before going inside the house, leaving the boy alone in the yard. I looked again at the address above the garage to make sure it matched what Ernesto had given me. I circled the block, and when I came back to the house, I didn't see the boy so I pulled to the curb. Though I'd little idea what I was doing at the house or what I thought I'd find, it hadn't even occurred to me that Murphy might have a family. The version of him I'd formed in my mind couldn't live in that house or be a husband and a father. My head filled with thoughts of the wreck, the little smashed SUV, the car seat, and the Life Flight helicopter leaving the scene. I looked over my shoulder at the bear and balloon in the backseat, and when I turned back the little boy had stepped out from behind the large oak tree in the yard. He held a yellow toy dump truck and was staring at me.

I suppose a shrink might call what happened next a kind of temporary mental break or something, and I'm not entirely sure that isn't what happened.

I rolled down my passenger side window. The little boy took a couple steps away from the tree, and now that I could see him better, I guessed him to be about six or so; he was a good-looking kid with dark hair and eyes, and I wondered if this was what Murphy looked like.

Because I didn't know what else to do, I waved. To my surprise he waved back and came toward my truck. "Cool truck you got there," I called through the window. The boy perked up.

"It's a Tonka. My daddy got it for me." The boy's voice was deeper and more assured than I expected.

"Mine's a Ford." I tapped hard on the dash with my hand. "Not a Tonka, but it gets the job done."

The boy looked at me and then at my rig for a moment. "What's it do?"

"Well," I said and took a quick look up and down the street. I didn't know what I was doing, but I knew people would be getting off work soon and my being there without a single dead car in sight probably didn't look good. I got out of my rig. "You wanna see how it raises up and down?" He nodded quickly. "There's a bunch of levers over here that work it," I said, but he didn't move.

"Okay," I said. "Stay clear." I raised the deck and extended it down to the street and then brought it back up. The boy's eyes went wide as he watched the hydraulics working. I kept an eye on the front window of the house. The curtains were open about halfway, but I didn't see any movement inside. "Pretty cool, huh?" I said after the deck was back in place.

The boy nodded again.

"My name's Howard," I said. "What's yours?"

The boy looked over his shoulder at his house as if he heard something, and I flinched and started to make for the cab, but he turned back to me and no one came out of the house.

"Alexander."

"Nice to meet you, Alexander." I knew even as I said that it sounded bad, but I had to ask, "Where's your mom and dad?"

"Mom's resting. Daddy's sick at the hospital."

"Oh," I said.

"What's that?" Alexander pointed into the cab of my truck. I got in and slid across and opened the passenger door for him to see. Alexander came and stood in the open space in front of the door.

"This here? It's a GPS computer to tell me where I am and where I need to go."

"Why do you need to know where you are?"

"I need to know where I am so I can know how to get where I'm going," I said and entered in my address. "See, here we are, and this dot here is where I live. Now I know how to get home." I waited a moment while Alexander looked at the GPS screen.

"Where's the hospital?"

I scrolled the GPS map and pointed to show him. "Here."

"Mom says I can't see Daddy yet. He's still too sick." Alexander looked over his shoulder again and then pulled himself up, his hand along the top and his knee on the edge of the seat, to get a better look inside my truck. I thought for a moment about Murphy, still alive in his hospital bed, and about this neighborhood, and his house, and his wife and his boy, and all the other things he probably had that I didn't and how he'd nearly pissed it away. Then I thought about the brand-new family he'd killed and looked at Alexander right in front of me, clueless as to what his father had done. I realized then that I could grab him and be gone before anyone knew. I saw how, with one simple act, I could take something that Murphy didn't deserve and ruin his life—or what was left of it. It'd ruin mine too, but at that moment I didn't care. And I'd be lying if I said I didn't, for that moment at least, seriously consider it.

Then Alexander said, "I like your balloon." Like a goddamn punch in the gut, it took everything out of me. He was just a little kid who thought his dad was sick in the hospital. This little glimpse of Murphy's life had fucked me up so much I hadn't even considered how this boy might feel or what it would've done to him if I'd taken him.

I reached into the backseat and pulled the bear and balloon up to the front so Alexander could see them. "It's a friend of mine's," I said. He slowly reached for the bear, and when I nodded, he took it in his arms and cuddled it against his chest.

I looked up in time to see Alexander's mother storming out the front door. She began screaming his name as she barreled across the yard, and startled, he dropped the bear on the seat before sliding out and running to his mother. For a split second I thought of getting the hell out of there as quickly as I could, but I was afraid she'd see the name of the towing company on the door. So instead, I tried to stay calm despite the watery feeling in my bowels. I slid across the seat and stepped out behind Alexander. His mother scooped him off the ground and held him tight, backpedaling several steps. She looked like a woman who had just seen the rest of her life, nearly husbandless and now childless, flash before her eyes.

"Ma'am, I'm a friend of Glenn's," I said as evenly as I could, trying as much to calm myself as her. "We used to work together. I was just showing Alexander here my truck."

Her eyes were wide and searching my face, and she was squeezing Alexander so tightly the veins in her forearms bulged.

"I heard about the . . . about what happened, and I just wanted to stop by and . . . I don't know," I said.

"We're fine," she said, breathing heavily. As she began to calm some now that Alexander was safely in her arms, I could see in her face how tired she was. She'd probably spent the last couple days in a hospital watching her husband cling to life. Seeing her there holding her son, I felt sick to my stomach for what I'd almost done. "We're *fine*. Just leave us. *Please*."

"Okay," I said and raised my hands to show I meant no offense and walked around the front of my rig. She'd turned and was quickly walking toward the front door as if she thought I might chase them. "Take care of that one," I said before I got in. "He's a good kid."

I didn't make it a mile before I had to pull over because I was shaking too much to grip the steering wheel. I'd been consumed by grief over the death of a baby I didn't know, and some misguided sense of justice had driven me to nearly kidnap a child. I looked at that goddamn bear with its smile and its "It's a Boy!" balloon and knew that I had to be rid of them, and there was only one place where they belonged.

When I got my shit together enough to drive, I circled back to Murphy's street and parked a few houses down. Before I could have any second thoughts, I snatched the bear and balloon off the seat and jumped out of my truck. I didn't want to draw any more attention to myself, so I didn't run; instead, I cut across Murphy's yard, tight-ass walking up to the porch.

My plan was to set the bear and balloon in front of the door and hightail it out of there. I imagined how, one day in the future, Murphy might find the bear and wonder where it came from, and maybe even ask Alexander about it. It wasn't much, I knew, but it was *something*. But as I sat them down, Alexander's face appeared in the front window, and though I know he saw me, his expression was blank, innocent. I worried he might call out for his mother, but he didn't move. I looked at him as long as I could stand it; I wanted him to understand I meant him no harm, that I only wanted him to have the bear and balloon, but I hated myself for using him this way. But there was no turning back now, so I did my best to smile at him. I turned to leave, and as I walked away, I trusted he'd wait until I was long gone before stepping outside to retrieve what was now his.

THE SPOILS

As designed, in the last twenty-seven games we hadn't come within twenty points of a win. Do you have any idea what it's like to show up and know absolutely—every game—that you are going to not just lose, but be embarrassed? That if you give 100 percent, you're *not* doing your job? That your job is, in fact, to play the stooge every single night? No, you can't know what it's like to look in the mirror in the locker room after one of these games. Have you ever considered that guys like us, we might have families and kids? That it's our *job*, that we're not just out there to entertain you? How about this: What am I supposed to tell my son when he asks what I do for a living? And then later, when he asks how come we never win? Ever thought of that? No, I'll bet you haven't. At the end of the day, it's not the losing that bothers me so much, it's the not playing the game hard. It's unnatural.

That's why tonight, at the designated moment at the start of the fourth quarter when I usually wait flat-footed for an inbound pass so Whirlybird Wilkenson can steal it and glide in for a fancy, behind-the-back, 360 dunk—there are moments like this in the game for each of us—I let my instincts take over and I stepped to the ball. When it hit my hands, I planted my foot and spun hard to my right without even thinking about my knee, and Wilkenson sprawled, skin squeaking across the hardwood. There was a collective *ooh* in the crowd; they must've thought it was part of the show. As I brought the ball up the court, I glanced quickly over my shoulder and saw Wilkenson look to the sidelines as he got up. Coach glared at me as I passed half-court, but in those few seconds I'd decided that for the rest of the game things were going to be different: I was going to play straight and take the game to the Trotters. And, since no one pays to see the world-famous Harlem Globetrotters play defense, all it took was a head fake and crossover to beat my man for a lay-in and an easy two, which gave me eight for the night, my usual quota. So why, in all the moments of all the games on the tour, did I choose tonight, this moment, to play? Because, in the silence before the opening of the fourth quarter, I heard, crystal clear, my wife's whistle. It's shrill and trilling and I'd recognize it anywhere; it's the same whistle she used when she watched me play in college. Tonight's game was the closest stop on the tour to where we live, and it was the only chance she and my son would have to see me play. She'd only seen me a handful of times while I was playing in Belgium, the last game being the one where I tore up my knee. And I wanted my son to see me out on the court at least once, even if it was like this, and even if he was still too young to remember it later. We don't get any allotted tickets, and there is no designated section for wives and families of the Generals, so I had no idea where she and my son were sitting. They had to make a three-hour drive, so I knew they'd probably be late, and I didn't even know if they were there until I heard her whistle.

Instead of heading back down the court, I stayed for a full-court press. Jerry, our other guard, didn't have a clue what I was doing, and he stopped at mid-court. The look on his face told me he thought he'd missed a cue, but he didn't. I'd officially gone off script. He hustled back, and with his help we trapped Billy Flash Gordon in the corner, and when he tried one of his little behind-the-back passes, I got a hand on it, deflecting it to Roland, our forward, who, looking as lost as Jerry, took it to the rim two-handed. For a second he looked like he'd just been caught stealing, and clearly he was worried about having dunked the ball. We'd been coached to play old-school, under-the-rim basketball, to leave the dunking to the Trotters. The crowd cheered, but it felt uneasy, like they weren't sure what to make of the last two possessions.

Coach called a time-out, perhaps the first unscheduled time-out called by the Generals in Harlem Globetrotters' history. Usually, the Trotters go off and do their thing—throw buckets of confetti on the crowd, give high fives and hugs to children, joke with the adults, pester the referees—but it looked to me like neither the Trotters nor the referees knew what was going on. Typically, Coach makes a show of bringing us all into a huddle around a clipboard, acting as if he's drawing up a play. "What the fuck was that, Marcus?"

Clearly, he was off the script now, too. His job was to play a mild, Disney kind of villain, taunting the Globetrotters and such, but nothing like this. A family of four sat behind our bench, and the mother's eyes went wide. The two kids, probably six or seven years old, didn't seem to notice; they had their eyes on the video board above. "Just trying to play some ball, Coach," I said and tipped my chin toward the family.

He glanced over his shoulder and cleared his throat. "Good. Good. Now, look here, men. I've got just the play," he said, and all of us huddled up. Using his dry-erase marker and board, he made bold sweeping marks and large Xs and said things like, "and then, Johnson, you'll set a screen here, and Davis, you'll be open for the easy three," and so on. The thing is, Ed—that's his real name, not the one you'd find in the program—doesn't know anything more about basketball than the casual fan. He's just another actor, really, following a script, collecting a paycheck like the rest of us.

The buzzer signaled the end of the time-out, and as we headed back to the court, Ed grabbed my shoulder and leaned in as if to impart some last-minute advice like he'd probably seen real coaches do. "You better cut that shit out," he said. "Don't forget which team you're on."

"Kiss my ass, Ed," I said, nodding my head and smiling as I walked away.

Normally I wouldn't talk to him like that, but I knew he couldn't take me out of the game. First, we only travel with eight players, and the only other two guys who can play guard, Nick and Austin, were both out of commission. Nick sprained his ankle two nights ago in Kansas City and was in street clothes for tonight's game, and Austin flew home for the birth of his child. Our extra man, Dennis, is a big man, pushing seven feet, and even Ed wouldn't put him in to play guard. Besides, Mr. Klotz, the owner of the Generals, never said we couldn't play. In fact, he publicly claims we try to win every game. Second, Ed was going to get ejected sometime in the next three minutes, so all I had to do was wait him out. Every fifth game he gets ejected in the fourth quarter, and I knew it was tonight because we went over it in our pregame meeting. He pretends to blow a gasket, slamming his clipboard on the floor and tossing a chair onto the court Bobby Knight–style. It's really something to see, Ed with his bright red bow tie and checked blazer stomping around in front of the bench and then leaving the court under a blanket of boos.

As I jogged back onto the court, I scanned the stands again for my wife but didn't find her. The game wasn't a sellout, but it was close. We get the best crowds in midsized Midwestern cities without pro teams. While I was looking up, Wilkenson bumped me hard with his shoulder. "How you gonna punk me like that?" he said. "Who you think you are?"

There's usually a little trash talk during the game, but it's G-rated and mostly for the fans. Basically, the Trotters make fun of us—hide the ball under the backs of our jerseys, pull our shorts down, run us all over the court doing crazy figure-eight ball-handling moves. It's all designed to make us look stupid. But this was different. Whirlybird didn't say this for anyone's benefit but mine. "An actor," I said and smiled. "Like you." He stepped up in my face; he's got a good four inches on me. "You gonna do this here, with all these kids watching." I spread my arms and shrugged my shoulders, and the crowd, the ones who were actually paying close attention, booed lightheartedly, though I wasn't sure if it was at him or me.

"That's how it's going to be, huh?" he said and backed away. "You think you got enough game?"

"Let's find out," I said.

Whirlybird laughed and waved his hand at me dismissively as he backpedaled to his side of the court.

As we set up for the Trotters to inbound the ball, I brought my teammates in for a quick huddle. "I'm playing. No bullshit the rest of the quarter."

"Goddamn it, Marcus," Jerry said, and he dropped his head.

Roland started to speak, "But what about—"

I reminded him, and everyone else, of Ed's impending ejection. "I'm just asking," I said looking up at the clock, "for six and a half minutes."

"I ain't getting fired over this shit," said Stu, our center.

If there had been time, I would have explained that if anything happened, I would take the heat, but the referee handed the ball to one of the Trotters and blew his whistle. When the ball came in, I stayed with my man. As much as I wanted my teammates on board, I wasn't going to let them keep me from taking it to the Trotters. As they worked the ball up court, I glanced at the rest of my guys and saw that while they weren't playing man-to-man, the defensive formation was tighter than usual.

They scored on a twelve-foot jumper, though they had to settle for it. We were easily able to get those points back, plus one, when Jerry drained a three. After the basket he had a spring in his step I'd never seen before, but when I tried to catch his eye, he looked away. For some reason (pride, perhaps? conditioning?), the Trotters still tried to pull their trick stuff—say what you want about them, they're committed showmen—but it doesn't work when the other team isn't a part of the act, even if it was just Jerry and me. In the next three possessions, the game sort of took hold of us, and even though a couple of the guys weren't exactly playing hard, they weren't playing along anymore. We found our rhythm, and I went into a kind of zone. I couldn't see the crowd, and the Trotters' red, white, and blue jerseys went fuzzy. The court spread out before me, and it felt like everyone but me was moving in slow motion. All I heard was the slap of the ball on the hardwood, and the squeak of my teammates' shoes as they cut and juked to get open. I hadn't been locked in like that since before I blew out my knee. We went on a 6–0 run and cut their lead to nine.

The Trotters must've finally figured out that we were not letting them have this one, that at least a couple of us did have enough "game," because they left the tricks behind and pushed the ball hard up the court. What else were they going to do, stop the game? That's not really an option, especially since thousands of fans had put down their hard-earned to see a "real" game. Go ahead, check for yourself. The Harlem Globetrotters do not participate in fixed basketball games. The Trotters are great players, there's no doubt about it, but they've gotten used to having the game handed to them each night. Us, we're the fundamental guys who go unnoticed in the shadows of the great players. Little has changed in that regard. But, sound fundamentals are one of the core requirements to be a General. That, and "to understand the role the Generals play in the Harlem Globetrotters' tour and that a game's final score doesn't always determine who wins." Tonight I was doing my best to change that.

After we picked off one of their lazy passes, they played defense, but it's been a long time since any of these guys had to defend for real. It had been a long time for us, too, but it seemed to come back more quickly. Jerry and I beat them down the court with a text-book give-and-go, and we cut the deficit to seven with just over four minutes to play. I stole a look at Ed pacing by our bench. It made for good theater; even the expression on his face. To an outsider he probably looked focused and concerned about how to win the game when what he was really worried about was what would happen if we actually pulled it off.

The Trotters slowed the pace of the game to burn up as much time from the clock as they could, but we got within five on a fadeaway jumper from Roland, and on his way back up the court he nodded at me. We gave up two when Hang-time Harris drove the lane for a dunk. Roland had his feet set and took the charge, but surprise, surprise, we didn't get the call. If we had, it might've been another first in Globetrotters' history. The blown call gave Ed the perfect opportunity to get tossed. I worried for a moment that he wouldn't go through with it, but he did, thrown chair and all. Considering his options, he probably figured getting tossed would only further distance himself from our growing coup. After Ed's ejection, the Trotters seemed to think they had the game won and couldn't help showboating and playing to the crowd, but we took advantage and scored five unanswered, two on a running floater from me and another three from Jerry, to bring the game within two.

If this were real basketball, we would've fouled the first Trotter to touch the ball on the inbounds and taken our chances with one of them at the line, or we would've double-teamed the guy inbounding the ball to try to get a five-second call, but that wasn't likely to happen given that the refs let the Globetrotters do pretty much whatever they wanted. No, we had to get a clean steal or force them to miss.

I gave Wilkenson room as he brought the ball up the court, and maybe he thought I was letting him have it, that I was finally back on script, that all of this was just to make the game exciting for the fans, because he went between his legs twice and around his back, his signature move: The Whirlybird. Maybe he just couldn't help himself. Maybe he thought his move was so good that it was impossible to defend, that all the nights he's beaten me with it were real. When he faked right and went left—he always goes left—I was right there and it was as if he handed the ball off to me. I raced down the court, and even though I knew I should let the rest of my team catch up, get set to play for the final shot, I couldn't wait. I set my feet behind the three-point line, and as I shot, I heard Wilkenson's feet pounding the court just over my shoulder. As the ball left my fingertips, I saw him in my periphery, lunging, trying to get a hand on the ball, but he was too late. He and I both watched the ball arc through the air and drop cleanly through the net. I listened hard for my wife's whistle in the silence that followed my shot, but I didn't hear it.

Down one with nine seconds on the clock, Whirlybird took better care of the ball this time as he brought it up the court, and I played tight, clean defense because I knew the refs would call even the slightest contact now. Why they didn't call a time-out, I don't know, but the Trotters moved the ball crisply around the perimeter trying to find the open man. I knew that Wilkenson was going to take the last shot, so I stuck to him. If we were going to lose, it was going to be because he beat me. The crowd counted down the seconds—*Five* . . . *Four* . . . *Three* . . . *Two*—and just before they got to *One*, Wilkenson stepped to a pass, set his feet, and went up for a jump shot. I got a hand directly in his face. Who knows how long it had been since he'd taken a shot under that kind of pressure? As the ball left his hand, the buzzer sounded and the entire arena went quiet while we watched his shot kick off the heel of the rim.

The crowd let out a collective groan and again went silent. Most of them just stood in their places, and it seemed they didn't know what to do, as if they thought the Globetrotters had one more gag in store for them, and this was part of it. We gathered in the center of the court, jumping up and down and mobbing each other, like we'd just won an NBA championship. Out of the corner of my eye, I saw several Globetrotters standing around, uncertain about what to do, and Whirlybird looked lost, like a boxer who's had a tough round and can't find his corner. Eventually they all headed to the tunnel in the corner of the arena. Despite what you might think, the Harlem Globetrotters have lost to the Generals before, six times in fact, but not since the '70s, so this current incarnation of the team had never lost. Until tonight.

When the booing started, I saw it beginning to sink in on my teammates' faces. We'd just defeated the mighty Harlem Globetrotters. What did this mean? Would we be fired? I have to admit, I hadn't planned on the kind of reaction we got from the fans. I would take the heat for all of it; I didn't want everyone let go because of some sudden, foolish sense of pride on my part. I'd been selfish, but my teammates stood by me.

As we went back to our bench—we don't have equipment managers to carry our warm-ups and water bottles—I saw the two kids in the front, the same two that belonged to the mother who heard Ed cuss during the time-out. The girl, looking up again at the video board, didn't seem to care what had happened. The boy, on the other hand, looked confused. His father had probably been telling him all about the world-famous Harlem Globetrotters ever since they got the tickets. Probably told him how much fun the game would be, how the Globetrotters would make spectacular shots and unbelievable slam dunks, and certainly that the Globetrotters would win. The Globetrotters always won. The boy looked so pathetic standing there clutching his souvenirs—a poster and plush red, white, and blue basketball—I wanted to go to him and tell him that what he'd just seen was something good, a triumph, a true victory, but I knew he couldn't understand what it meant to have done what we did. I thought then about my son. He was much too young to comprehend what happened, but if he wasn't, would he understand *why* I did it?

Behind the kids, all the way to the press boxes, fans were yelling and booing. I even saw a few balled-up hot dog wrappers rain down. Clearly, they couldn't appreciate it, either. Should I have expected any different? After I quickly picked up my stuff, I nodded at the children to try to convey to them, the best I could, that I was aware of what I'd done.

Usually, on our way to the tunnel a few fans will hang over the railing to shake our hands and tell us we played a good game, or to tell us to hang in there, that we'll "Get 'em next time," but tonight, no one was sticking around to congratulate us, and the ones hanging over the railing were angry. A couple of the guys on the team ran into the tunnel, and I don't blame them. I would have run if I were them, too. But this, whatever it was, was all on me.

"You got lucky, Twenty-two!" someone shouted. Though my name is in the program, no one even bothered to look it up.

"I want my money back, asshole!"

"You guys are just a bunch of bums! You don't deserve to win!"

Just before I went into the tunnel, I thought I heard my wife's whistle and I stopped. I cocked my head but the sound was gone, if it was ever there, and someone from above dumped their soda on me. The pieces of ice bounced off my head and shoulders and broke apart when they hit the floor. Someone else, taking a cue from the first guy, poured the dregs of his beer over my head. I stopped and looked up at the people at the railing above, but I didn't say anything. I stood there a winner, waiting for what I had coming to me.